TOO SOON FOR JEFF

Also by Marilyn Reynolds:

Telling

Detour for Emmy

TOO SOON FOR JEFF

Marilyn Reynolds

Morning Glory Press

Buena Park, California

Copyright © 1994 by Marilyn Reynolds

All Rights Reserved

Library of Congress Cataloging-in-Publication Data
Reynolds, Marilyn, 1935-
   Too soon for Jeff / Marilyn Reynolds.
      p.   cm.
   Summary: High school senior Jeff Browning is upset
when he learns that his girlfriend is pregnant. He is determined not to let a baby ruin his plans to go to college on a
debate scholarship, but his feelings change after the baby is
born.
   ISBN 0-930934-90-3 : $15.95.   -- ISBN 0-930934-91-1
(pbk.) : $8.95
   [1. Teenage fathers--Fiction. 2. Teenage parents--Fiction.
3. Parent and child--Fiction.] I. Title.
PZ7.R3373To   1994
[Fic.]--dc20   94-7585
                                                             CIP
                                                             AC

MORNING GLORY PRESS, INC.
6595 San Haroldo Way   Buena Park, CA 90620
Telephone 714/828-1998
FAX 714/828-2049
Printed and bound in the United States of America

To Doug Campbell
and the debaters of San Gabriel High School
and to Mimi Avocada

Acknowledgments

For sharing their insight and comments on this novel in progress, I thank:

Barry Barmore and the students at Century High School.

Mike Reynolds and Doug Campbell and their students at San Gabriel High School, especially Ali and Eric.

Judy Heitzenrader and Marilyn Mallow of Alhambra School District.

My colleagues in writing, Betty Haggerty, Dorothy Hole, Jeanne Leiter, and Jill Morgan.

Assorted kind readers including Cindi Foncannon, Matthew Reynolds, Sharon Reynolds-Kyle, Liz McDonald, and Marg Dodson.

A special thank you is due Ginger Rouse, patient educator for maternal child health at Garfield Hospital, Alhambra, California, and fellow writer Anne Scott for close readings and discerning critiques regarding the world of Jeff Browning.

I am grateful to Kathy and Joe Harvey for supporting the arts by providing the perfect writing retreat setting, and to Jeanne Lindsay of Morning Glory Press for her careful attention to all phases of this process, and for her openness, encouragement, and general respect for the muse.

Marilyn Reynolds

"We're going to have a baby," she said, smiling the half-smile I once thought was so cute.

I couldn't believe what I'd heard.

"What?"

"We're going to have a baby."

Not, I'm pregnant, or we've got a problem, but we're going to have a baby.

"You're kidding. Right?"

"I got a pregnancy test to be sure. I didn't want to tell you until I knew for certain," she said, smiling all lovingly at me. "It's due in July. A little baby from us, together."

CHAPTER

1

My name is Jeff Browning. I'm seventeen years old, and I've got problems.

Here's the thing. Last night Christy and I were sitting in my car, in front of her house. It's February, and cold for Southern California, and the car windows were steamed over by the warmth of our breathing. Any other time it would have felt safe and cozy, sitting all closed in. But I wasn't feeling cozy last night. I was tense and nervous.

It was late, and I was trying to get up the nerve to break up with Christy. I was determined to do it before the night was over, but it was difficult to get any of those breaking-up words out of my mouth.

Christy and I have been together for so long, and we've been through so much . . . laughter, tears, all that stuff you see in the movies and think will never happen to you until it does . . . It's hard. I don't want to hurt her, I'm just tired of feeling tied.

Christy always keeps track of our month anniversaries, which we count from the first time I kissed her, September 17, seventeen months ago. We were at the annual back-to-debate team party at my friend Dashan's house. I'd noticed Christy (Christina Calderon) in my debate class, but I hadn't really talked to her. She was a freshman and I was a junior. She seemed older—innocent, though. Not like some of those little ninth grade chicks that look about thirty and you think if you even talk to them you could pick up some kind of disease.

Christy has long, black hair, sort of medium-dark skin, and light green eyes. When I first looked into those eyes, I thought she must be wearing some kind of fake colored contacts. I didn't know God ever handed out such beautiful eyes. I thought you'd have to buy them at some store.

Me, I'm kind of average looking, brown hair, brown eyes, light skin, about five foot ten. Christy sometimes calls me handsome, joking around, but really I'm just ordinary looking.

Anyway, we've been together ever since that party. In a way you could say it was first love for both of us. Christy had never been with a guy before me, and I hadn't ever really loved anyone. I wasn't a virgin. There had been two girls along the way I'd liked a lot, but I'd never thought I was in love before. It was different with Christy and things were good with us for a long time—really good. Then something changed.

Last summer I visited my grandmother in Florida, like always, and I met this girl, Beth. We didn't do anything, it wasn't like that. But we laughed a lot.

She was my age. Maybe that made me realize how immature Christy can be at times. Beth wasn't always upset about her family, or needing me to tell her how cute she was, or to take her somewhere. She could take care of herself. I liked that.

Part of the thing with Christy was that she really depended on me. Her family life was messed up. Her dad is one of these super bossy guys who thinks he's god of the family and everyone in it. I felt sorry for her, having to put up with him all the time. She envied me, living in a house where people don't yell at each other all the time.

When her dad was on the rampage, she'd walk to a pay phone and I'd come get her. He wasn't violent, but he could be very mean and nasty all the same. Then, sometimes he was nice.

I never knew, when I went to see Christy, if I was going to see the nice Mr. Calderon, or the mean Mr. Calderon. I liked it better if I didn't see Mr. Calderon at all. Anyway, Christy spent a lot of time at my house because things are relaxed there.

Besides having a screwed-up family life when Christy first came to Hamilton High, she hardly had any friends there. She'd gone to Catholic schools before that, and most of her friends had gone on to Mission High School. So I guess she was kind of lonely.

Don't get me wrong, I'm not the most popular guy at Hamilton High, but I've lived here all my life and gone to school with a lot of the same people since kindergarten. Between school, Little League and AYSO, I know practically everyone. So I helped Christy get a social life and I gave her a shoulder to cry on when her dad was acting like a butthole, which was most of the time.

Anyway, while I was in Florida last summer, I missed Christy. But when I got back, my feelings had changed. I hadn't meant for them to, it just happened. On the outside everything looked the same. We still hung around together all the time. I still liked sex with her—a lot. But where it used to make me feel important that she needed me to sort of take care of her, now sometimes I felt all closed in.

When I said I wanted to go out with the guys on Friday nights, she'd ask, "What am I supposed to do when you're out partying with your homeboys?"

"I didn't say partying, Christy. I just want to hang out with my friends sometimes."

"And leave me stuck at home watching reruns with my family? You know I hate being home on a Friday night."

"Well, you could go out with some of *your* friends. What

about Kim? You could go to a movie or something." Kim is
her friend from St. Catherine's, and days and most nights
they talk for hours on the phone. Was it unreasonable to
think they might get together now and then on a Friday
night?

But Christy didn't think much of that suggestion. She
said, "Kim and John go out every Friday night. *He* always
wants to be with *her*."

"It's not that I don't want to be with you . . ."

"I don't understand," she'd said, her green eyes filling
with tears. "You're the only one I ever want to be with . . .
I like Kim, but I *love* you," she'd whispered, and then kissed
me long and full.

One thing led to another, and I forgot about going out
with the boys. I must be crazy to want to change things, I'd
thought, lying beside her, feeling close to her in the warm
afterglow of sex. But the next afternoon, when she'd asked
me to come get her and take her back to my house because
her sister and dad were yelling and screaming at each
other, I got that trapped feeling all over again. Life can be
very confusing.

For a while I thought I'd take the easy way out, stay with
her for the rest of the school year and then we'd just
naturally drift apart when I go away to college. Going away
to college has been a dream of mine for a long time.

My mom and grandma have each been putting money in
a savings account for my college education ever since my
dad left. But between that money and the money I've saved
working at the Fitness Club, there's barely enough for
tuition and books at a state school. The bad news is there
won't be anything left to pay for room and board away from
home. But here's the *really* good news. I almost for sure am
getting a debate scholarship to a small college in Texas, so
I can actually live away from home, in a dormitory, like in
the TV sitcoms.

Mr. Rogers, my debate teacher, helped me a lot, but I've worked hard for it too. It's sort of a dream come true. All I have to do is qualify for nationals this year, and the scholarship is mine. I'll compete in two events, Dramatic Interpretation and Policy Debate. I already know pretty much what I'm doing for both events. I just need to polish the rough edges between now and March.

My partner in Policy Debate, Jeremy, is probably getting a scholarship to U.C. Berkeley. He may be getting one to Yale, too, only that would be in science. Jeremy is extremely intelligent. Trin, too, may get a debate scholarship. We've got a really hot debate program at Hamilton High.

Anyway, back to me and Christy. It's tempting just to stay with her until I go away to college, but that feels like living a lie. Besides, I'm sort of interested in someone else and I think she may be interested in me, too. Not like it's another serious love, but it might be fun to hang out with this other girl now and then.

So there I was last night, sitting with Christy in the car, in front of her house, trying to get up the nerve to break up with her. I'd practiced the words so many times—we'll always be friends, I'll always care about you, but I can't be with you anymore—or—if we try being apart for a while, then we'll know whether or not we really love each other.

"Christy . . ." I started, my heart pounding. Why was it so hard?

"I have something to tell you, Jeff," she said.

"I have something to tell you, too," I said, hoping we each wanted to tell each other the same thing. No luck.

"We're going to have a baby," she said, smiling the half-smile I once thought was so cute.

I couldn't believe what I'd heard.

"What?"

"We're going to have a baby."

Not, I'm pregnant, or we've got a problem, but we're going to have a baby.

"You're kidding. Right?"

How could she be pregnant when we'd always been so careful?

She dug around in her purse for a piece of paper, then handed it to me. I turned on the inside light and read a notice from a family clinic—her name was on it, and the box for "positive pregnancy" was checked. I kept staring at the paper, not believing my eyes.

"I got a pregnancy test to be sure. I didn't want to tell you until I knew for certain," she said, smiling all lovingly at me. "It's due in July. A little baby from us, together."

"But you're on the pill. How can you be pregnant?"

"Things happen sometimes," she said, her smile fading.

"And July?" I counted on my fingers, February to July. "You're already four months pregnant and you're just now telling me?"

"I told you, I waited to be sure."

"You also told me the pill was ninety-nine percent effective."

"Well, maybe we're the one percent."

"God!"

"Maybe I forgot to take it sometimes," she said, looking away. "I don't know. All I know is, I went to the clinic and we're going to have a baby."

"Forgot to take it sometimes? Are you telling me that all these months you've supposedly been on the pill you were only sort of on the pill?"

"Don't yell at me. You know I can't stand to be yelled at. Don't start acting like my dad!"

"Christy! We can't have a baby! We've got lots of things we have to do before either of us has a kid. I mean, what kind of parents could we be? *We're* still kids!"

"You'll be eighteen next month. That's an adult!"

I turned off the light and sat slumped behind the steering wheel, staring at the fogged-over windshield.

"Christy, we can't possibly have a baby. We're still in high school."

"Lots of people still in high school have babies. Look at Phillip and Susan," she said.

"You look at them! They've both practically quit school. Phil is working his butt off at McDonald's—assistant manager. Wow! And Susan's always complaining about the baby this and the baby that. I'm going to college next year, I'm not going to work full-time at some fast-food place so I can buy diapers!" I knew I was talking loud, but God, she was pregnant?

"You wouldn't have to work at a fast-food place. They're always asking you to work more hours at the Club. That's a good job."

"I don't want more hours at the Fitness Club. I want to go away to college next year. It's what I've always planned on doing and it's what I'm going to do."

Christy sat silently, turned away from me. Finally she asked, "What did you want to tell me?"

"What?"

"You said you had something to tell me, too."

"Oh," I said. "It was nothing."

How could I tell her I wanted to break up, when she'd just told me she was pregnant? That changed everything.

We were both quiet for a long time, thinking our own thoughts, I guess. Then I pulled her close to me and rubbed her back, the way I always did when she was upset or sad.

"We'll work this out," I whispered. "I'll take you back to the clinic on Monday. We'll get set up for an abortion. It's not too late."

"Abortion!" she screamed, pushing me away. "You want to kill our baby?"

"Don't be so dramatic! It's not a baby, it's a mass of cells, probably not even as big as a chicken egg."

She put her hands over her face. "You said you wanted kids," she sobbed.

"I didn't mean now! God, Christy, you know I've always

planned to go to college. And what about your plans to be an audiologist and help deaf kids? Teen mothers do not go to college!"

"Some do," she said. "I will."

"Oh, come on, Christy . . . Look at Susan's life since she had the baby. She's out of school as much as she's in—the baby has a fever, the baby's cutting teeth. Get real. How will you possibly go to college and start a career if you have a little baby that needs your constant attention?"

"Maybe our moms would help take care of it. And we could take turns. It would be fun. There's that extra bedroom at your house that's not even being used. It could be a perfect room for a baby."

"Well that's not for me! And I don't think my mom would be all excited about turning her study into a baby's room. I don't think your mom is going to be jumping up and down with excitement over this news, either. And your dad! He'll go nuts!"

"You can just talk to him, like you did when he wouldn't let us go out. Remember?"

"Geez, Christy. This is a slightly bigger deal than going to a movie, you know?"

God. Pregnant? How could this be? We'd been so careful! I couldn't end up like Phillip! I wanted to be *less* tied down, not *more*! I felt dizzy, closed in. I couldn't breathe! The car was getting smaller and smaller. I jumped out, slammed the door and started walking, fast, down the street, feeling the dampness of the misty night on my face and in my hair. How could this have happened to me?

Always I'd used condoms. That was something I was very careful about, even the first time, when I was fifteen and fumbling all over the place. But a few months ago, when Christy said she'd gone on the pill because of being irregular or something, well . . . it was a lot easier. And we didn't worry about AIDS, or other diseases, because we were only with each other.

I walked faster, past the house on the corner with the huge oak tree in front. There was a big yellow plastic slide under the tree, and a treehouse with a rope ladder leading up to it where I'd often seen kids playing. I wasn't ready to build treehouses! I didn't want a kid!

I broke into a run, across the street, one block, two, to the big Safeway near where Christy and I used to park after school, when we were first getting to know each other. I leaned against the wall, breathing hard.

What should I do? What could I do? I didn't want the responsibility of a kid! Her parents would kill me if they found out. And my mom? God, I didn't know what she'd say. I was so young the first time she talked to me about the importance of rubbers that I thought it had something to do with keeping my feet dry.

My mom is studying to be a nurse and she's a fanatic about safe sex. She's always coming home from her nursing classes with horror stories about AIDS and other STDs. She has two slogans that she's been preaching to me for about forever. Never ever have meaningless sex, and never have sex without a condom unless you're ready to get sick and/or take on the responsibilities of fatherhood.

I stood, still leaning against the market, shivering against the cold stucco. Maybe it was a mistake. Doctors make mistakes all the time.

The security guard sauntered over, carrying a billy club in his right hand.

"No loitering here," he said.

"It's a public place," I said.

"Not now it ain't. We're closed."

I felt like punching the phony smile off his ugly face. But I'm not the kind of guy who does stupid stuff like that. I turned and walked slowly away, toward Christy's house. She wasn't in the car when I got back. I stood outside for a while, looking at her lighted bedroom window, then got in my car and drove home.

As I started the turn into my driveway I shut off the lights and the engine, and coasted slowly to the place in front of the garage where I always park my car. The light was on in my mom's study, and I knew if I went in while she was still awake she'd want to talk. I wasn't up to it. Just thinking about how disappointed my mom would be if she knew Christy was pregnant made my stomach feel all fluttery, the way it used to get when I first started competing in debate tournaments.

It's weird how one minute things seem to be one way, and the next minute everything's changed. Someone tells you something, and the world you thought you knew is all different. That's how I felt the morning my dad walked into my bedroom and told me he wouldn't be living with us any more. And that's how I felt sitting in my driveway last night, like the world had taken a big turn, and it was a turn I didn't like, and nothing I could do would turn it back.

I sat watching my house, listening to the police copter circling overhead, waiting for Mom to go to bed. I've lived in the same house for as long as I can remember—a basic three-bedroom two-bath house with an attached garage. It's not fancy or anything, not like some of the houses up in the Highlands area of Hamilton Heights. But it's not a neighborhood where people have to put iron bars on their windows either.

For awhile after my dad left, he was bugging my mom to sell our house and rent an apartment, so he could get his money out of the place. Mom said they owed it to me to give me a decent place to live, in a decent neighborhood.

"I'm not making one more payment on this place," he'd said. That's the kind of person he is. Once he decided to leave, he couldn't care less about the people he left behind.

Mom told him, "So don't make another payment. But we're staying in the house." That was when she started working for Town and Country Realty.

I guess it's been a good place to grow up: 1264 Columbus Street, Hamilton Heights, California. But even though it looked exactly the same as it always had, if Christy really was pregnant, nothing would ever be the same again.

Finally, after I'd been sitting in the driveway for about 20 minutes, all the lights went out except for the ones on the back porch and in my bedroom. I stayed in my car a few more minutes, then tiptoed quietly inside.

CHAPTER

2

"You're awake kind of early this morning, aren't you?" my mom says, not looking up as I walk past the door of the bedroom/study on my way to the kitchen.

She's sitting at her big oak desk, gazing at her computer screen. A microbiology book is open before her. This is how I've found her every Sunday for the last three years. She's studying to be a registered nurse—it's what she's wanted for a long time.

Mom quit college after her first year so she could work and help my dad get through school. Then I came along. Her plan was to go back to school when I started first grade, but by that time my dad had left us and she had to work full time just to make ends meet. Real estate is not great in Southern California right now, but she's been in the business long enough that people know her and trust her, so she does okay. Anyway, she's always been interested in medical stuff and in helping people, so when I started high school and could be more on my own, she started taking classes at Hamilton Heights City College.

"Well, *aren't* you up early?" she repeats, looking up from her book now.

"Couldn't sleep," I say.

"Worried about something?" She gives me one of those intense looks like she can see inside me. I swear, I don't know why my mom needs to study nursing in order to get out of real estate. She should just open a little mind reading parlor.

"What's the trouble?"

"No trouble," I lie, hoping there's some mistake and Christy isn't really pregnant, or if she is, she'll decide to get an abortion after all. No need to get my mom all wigged out over something that may not even be a problem.

"How are things with you and Christy these days?" she asks.

"Fine," I say.

"School?"

"Fine."

"How's your Dramatic Interpretation piece coming?"

"Fine."

"How are things at the Fitness Club—your boss treating you okay?"

"Fine."

She looks at me for a while, like she wants to hear more from me than "fine," then goes back to her studies.

When I was little, my mom and I were real tight. I was only five when my dad split, and I guess when he stopped loving my mom, he stopped loving me, too. It seemed that way anyway, because I sure didn't see much of him after that.

He was supposed to take me every other weekend, but usually something came up. So really, it was just me and my mom, and I pretty much told her everything. I knew I could depend on her. She was never too busy for me. She even coached my Little League team one year. She did a good job, too. She's cool. Sometime around junior high school though, I stopped telling her all of my business. I mean, we still talked and everything, but I had a private side, too.

I pour some grape-nuts in a bowl, slice a banana over it,

it, cover the whole thing with milk and lean against her doorway, slurping my breakfast.

"What did you do last night, Ma?" I say, figuring if we talk about her night, we won't be talking about mine.

"Went to a movie."

"How was it?"

"Fine."

"Who'd you go with?"

"May."

"How's she?"

"Fine."

I glance up to see if she's making fun of me. She is. I can tell by the barely turned up corners of her mouth. My mom still looks pretty good for thirty-eight, except her hair is already totally grey. But she's not fat, like Benny's mom. All my friends like her because, for one thing, she's got a sense of humor, and for another, she keeps a well-stocked refrigerator. The refrigerator is another reason Christy likes being at my house more than she likes being at her own. I guess I'm lucky to have a mom like mine, and not to be living with my dad, who is a jerk, but not as big a jerk as Christy's.

By the time I get to the Fitness Club to start work, I feel better. The whole thing is probably some big mistake. Or maybe Christy was just playing a joke on me. She's been acting kind of weird lately. But no, she was really upset last night, that part was for sure. Probably we'll find out it's a mistake. We never did it without a condom until after she'd been on the pill for over a month. And once a condom broke, but that was way last year. It's got to be a mistake.

"**H**ey, why so serious this morning?" It's Faye, this old woman who had a stroke about a year ago.

"Hi, Faye," I say. "Want some help?"

"Of course. I'll do anything to get your attention," she says with a laugh.

She starts her training circuit. I adjust seats and weights for her as she makes her rounds. When she first started coming to the club, she had to use a walker and she couldn't manage any weight at all. After a few months she had increased both the weights and repetitions on each exercise and she could walk with just the help of a cane. It's been so amazing watching Faye's progress that sometimes I think it'd be cool to be a physical therapist. I'm pretty sure I'll stay with my plan to be a teacher, though. Faye is inspiring, but so is Mr. Rogers.

Besides being a tough old lady, Faye's a big joker. Like today. When I lean over to bring the pulley bar down to her she reaches up and pats me on the cheek.

"If I were ten years younger I could sure go for you."

I laugh. If she were ten years younger she'd be sixty-eight.

"I promise it would be safe sex," she says.

"I think you should go for Mr. Sampson," I say, not wanting to think at all about the safety, or danger, of sex.

"Sampson's older than God," she says.

"But he can outlast almost anyone on the stairmaster."

"Not my type. You're my type," she says. "Rent that movie *Harold and Maude* and give it some thought," she tells me.

Faye banters her way through her whole workout, then walks, leaning on her cane in a lopsided way, toward the showers. I admire her for how hard she's worked, and how she can always find something to laugh about.

After Faye leaves I stand gazing out the window toward the San Gabriel mountains, convincing myself everything's going to be fine. The clouds have lifted and the sun on the peaks is shiny and glistening. No smog today. Some days it's so smoggy I can't even see the outline of the mountains from here, but today I can see individual trees clear up at the top, and roads that from this distance look like narrow trails.

It's slow around the club on Sunday afternoons—mainly

only dedicated muscle men with bulging biceps and pulsing veins. Those guys don't need help or guidance from me.

"Ugh!" I turn quickly, startled by a punch in the ribs.

"Steve!" I return the punch.

"Hey, watch it. Don't be hard on your old uncle."

He laughs this high-pitched, funny laugh that always gets me going, too. Benny, my friend from before kindergarten who has the fat mom, says when Steve laughs all the dogs in the neighborhood start howling.

"What's up?" he says.

"The sky," I say. It's a ritual we've had since I was a little kid. It's not really funny anymore, but we still always say it. Steve is my mom's brother, and in some ways he's been kind of like a dad to me.

"When do you get off work?"

"Four," I say.

"How about I do a quick workout, then you and me go grab a garbageburger and onion rings down at Barb and Edie's?"

"Sounds good. I'm starving."

"Me, too," Steve says, stepping up on the treadmill and starting his jogging routine.

Barb and Edie's is this little dumpy place across from the furniture warehouse down on Fifth Street. It doesn't look like much, but it's got the best and biggest hamburgers I've ever seen. Two huge meat patties (not like those thin pressed hockey-puck things you get at the golden arches), cheese, lettuce, guacamole, onions, tomatoes, and a great secret sauce. The first time I ever ate a whole garbageburger was almost as big a deal as when I got my driver's license. Steve and I go there a lot. It's run by these two really gruff women, Barb and Edie, of course. The worst thing about it is that there's always country music blasting from the juke box, but that's a small sacrifice to make for the sake of a garbageburger and the best onion rings in all of L.A. County.

I step out to the hallway, pick up the phone, and dial

Christy's number. Her twelve-year-old sister, Maria, answers.

"Is Christina there?" I ask.

"No."

"Do you know when she'll be back?"

"No."

"Where'd she go?"

"None of your business. How come you got in a fight?"

"What makes you think we got in a fight?"

"'Cause . . . She was a real witch this morning. She always picks on me when she's mad at you."

"Well, tell her I called anyway, will you?"

"Why should I?"

"Don't then," I say, hanging up the phone. Maria is a total brat.

I go back to the workout room and start wiping down the exercise bikes and weights. I hear the steady rhythm of Steve's Nikes hitting the treadmill. I can tell by listening that he's running at about seven miles an hour.

I catch his reflection in one of the floor to ceiling mirrors they have over by the stretching area. Sweat is dripping from his face. His wet tee shirt is plastered to his back. For a thirty-three-year-old guy he does pretty good. I like my Uncle Steve a lot. I wonder what he'd think, if he knew I'm worried about Christina being pregnant.

When I was little, after my dad left but I was still expecting him to come around, I was really sad and lonely. And I was mad at my mom. My mom's always been a nice person, but I thought if she'd been just a little nicer, maybe my dad wouldn't have left us. And I was mad at Benny and Jeremy because their dads *hadn't* left them. Mostly I was mad at myself because if I'd been a better son, then for sure my dad would have stayed with us. I'd remember when he got mad at me for leaving my bike in the driveway, or for spilling my milk at dinner time, and I'd know for sure it was all my fault.

But even when I was the saddest six-year-old in the world, my Uncle Steve could make things better. I remember this one Sunday—sitting on the porch, waiting for my dad to show up. He'd promised to take me to his company picnic. I had my baseball and glove beside me, ready to go. Steve was helping my mom paint her bedroom. When the phone rang, I covered my ears. I knew what I'd be hearing. Mom came out and sat down beside me taking my hands away from my ears.

"Daddy can't make it today after all," she said. She tried to hug me, but I pushed her away. I didn't want to cry. Maybe she'd misunderstood, and he'd be there any minute, and I didn't want him to see my eyes all red, like a little baby's. I stayed out on the porch for hours, I guess. Finally, Uncle Steve came out and sat beside me. He handed me a can of soda, and opened one for himself. He sat there with me for a long time.

"It's not your fault, you know," he said.

I remember that time like it was yesterday. How it felt to be six, little, but safe under my uncle's arm, and understood. I can still feel the afternoon cooling air, and see the bright purple blossoms of the jacaranda trees that lined our block. That was the beginning of knowing who I could depend on—who really loved me, and who didn't. I never counted on my dad showing up after that day. When he did, I went, and when he didn't, I found something else to do. I stopped letting it matter. Early in my life I promised myself that I would never, no matter what, disappoint my kid the way my dad had disappointed me. I'm not ready to start keeping any promises about kids though. Not yet.

At 3:45 I call Christy again, and again Maria answers.

"She doesn't want to talk to you," Maria says in a sing-songy voice.

"Is she there?"

"Wouldn't you like to know?"

I hang up. I'll stop by her house after Steve and I get a bite to eat. It will be better to talk to her in person, anyway. But she's probably not pregnant. Things always seem worse late at night and real early in the morning. Now, in the light of day, I'm pretty sure everything's going to be all right.

No more sex without a condom, though. No more depending on this pill business. Really, I've got to stop having sex with Christy, no matter what. Make a clean break. It's not fair to either one of us to be together but not happy anymore. I've got to work this thing out, be honest, get it over with.

CHAPTER

3

After we pig out on garbageburgers and onion rings, with two sodas each, Steve invites me back to his place to watch *The Unforgiven* with him.

"I guess not," I say. "I've got homework due tomorrow. Besides, I've seen it about ten times."

"You can't get too much of Clint Eastwood," Steve says. He loves Clint Eastwood movies. My mom is a Tracy/Hepburn fan. Me, I watch whatever comes along.

Steve and I walk to the parking lot together, then go our separate ways.

My Uncle Steve is the kind of guy who for sure should have had kids. He and his wife, Janie, wanted kids but she never got pregnant. They were all set to adopt a little boy when Janie found a lump in her breast. Then it was surgery and chemotherapy. It was awful. She'd always been full of life, laughing and joking around, like Steve. But then we watched her waste away.

She died about four years ago. Poor Janie. And poor Uncle Steve. At first he stayed home all the time, looking at pictures and touching her clothes. He told me once he liked to smell her shoes, like it proved she'd really been there. I didn't know whether to laugh or cry, or get out of there. I think I just stood and looked at him like he was some kind of freak. Anyway, he's better now, but I think he still misses Janie a lot.

I swing past Christy's house. Kim's car is parked out front and she and Christy are sitting in it. Kim is an aide in the Hearing Impaired program, too. It really annoys me when they sit around and use sign language and I have no idea what they're saying, except that I'm sure it's about me. But the worst thing is how Christy tells Kim our personal business. I wouldn't be surprised if Christy told Kim she was pregnant before she even told me.

I park behind them, walk to Christy's side of the car, and lean down to talk to her. She won't look at me.

"Christy," I say. "I've been trying to call you all day."

She says nothing.

"Can we talk?"

Nothing. Kim doesn't look at me either.

"Come on, Christy. I just want to talk to you."

She rolls the window up.

I walk to my car, get in, slam the door, and peel out. Damn she ticks me off!

Monday morning, when I go out to my car to leave for school, there is a letter tucked under the windshield wiper. I get in and read it. It is from Christy.

> *Dear Jeff: I don't know how you can be so cruel, to want to kill our baby. You said you would always love me and now you want to kill a life we've made together, and leave an unhappy soul to haunt us forever. I never thought you would be like that. Love, Christy*

I sit for a long time, thinking. It's true, I did say I'd always love her. I'd said it lots of times. And I meant it, too, when I said it. But I hadn't said it since I got back from

Florida. Since then, I'd said I loved her, but not that I would *always* love her. And even back when I thought I would always love her, I never said let's hurry up and have a baby!

I stuff the letter in my glove compartment, then drive to Jeremy's house. He's sitting on the curb reading, with about ten books stacked beside him. Jeremy's in these honors classes where he's already getting college credit. He's a brain, but I like him anyway.

"Hey, J.B., whassup?"

"Not much," I say, reaching across and opening the door for him. I'm J.B., Jeremy's J.J., for Jeremy Jackson, and Benny's B.D. for Benny Dominguez. Those nicknames got started in preschool, when everybody had their initials pasted on their cubbies. The three of us probably wouldn't be friends if we'd just met in high school, because we're so different. But, because we were tight from sandbox days, through G.I. Joes, to finding out exactly what it was that adults did to get babies, we still hang together some. Jeremy and I are really tight because we do all that debate stuff together. Benny—sometimes Benny gets kind of crazy, but he's still my friend anyway.

We drive on to Benny's, where we sit in the driveway and wait, as always. Finally, Benny comes running out of his house, hair wet, pulling his tee shirt on, and jumps into the back seat.

"Hey, Dudes," he says.

"Hey, B.D.," Jeremy says.

Benny pokes me on the back of the head.

"Hey, I said hey."

"Hey, Benny," I say, without enthusiasm.

"Hey, did you guys see that dude on TV last night?"

That's how Benny is—fifty channels on his TV and he thinks we know exactly what dude he's talking about.

"Who?" Jeremy asks.

"This dude, Man. He was hanging from his teeth, under this airplane while they flew in circles over some city."

"Missed it," Jeremy says.

"You should have seen it, Jer. How about you, Jeff, did you catch it?"

"No."

"What's wrong with you guys? Watchin' 'Sixty Minutes' with your moms or something?"

We pull into the parking lot, get our stuff out, and walk toward class. Well, Jeremy and I get our stuff. Benny's always empty handed. When textbooks are handed out in September, B.D. puts them all in his locker. Then, in June, he takes them out and hands them back to his teachers. He says he's saving the taxpayers money because he keeps all of his books in pristine condition.

I'm somewhere between Jeremy and Benny as far as school is concerned. I work pretty hard, because I want to go to college. English and history are okay, but sometimes I really have to sweat over math and science.

Debate is my thing, though, especially Dramatic Inter-pretation—D.I. is what we call it. I was surprised when I found out I was good at it, in the ninth grade.

Benny was good, too. Really, he was great at Humorous Interpretation, but he couldn't be bothered with going to tournaments, so Rogers dropped him from the program last year.

As for Jeremy, he can look at the cover of a book and practically know everything that's inside. He'll for sure go to some big-name university. Berkeley or Yale or Harvard—these aren't for me. But neither are failed classes with summer school make-ups.

Benny's been going to summer school since the sixth grade to make up failed classes. Sometimes when he aims for "D"s, he shoots too low.

My mom says that after high school our three lives will go in different directions, and we'll drift apart. I don't think so. I think we'll always be really good friends. But then, I thought I would always love Christy, too, and right now I wish I'd never met her. I know that sounds cold, but I'm trying to tell an honest story here.

Fifth period I walk into the debate class and take my regular seat. There are no assigned seats here, but everybody usually sits in the same place anyway. I don't know why. Sometimes Mr. Rogers complains, tells us to get out of our ruts, mix it up a bit. Really—"Mr. Rogers?" But he's practically the opposite of the TV guy. He's a lot more cynical, and he's sloppy. He never wears anything but beat-up jeans and a faded tee shirt, even to open house. "It's a beautiful day in the neighborhood . . ." we sing sometimes, to annoy him. If we keep it up long enough he ends up throwing erasers at us and banging his head against the chalkboard.

We joke around a lot in this class, but I think I've learned more in here than in any other class. Rogers is always trying to get us to think for ourselves, not just believe something because he says so. He never pulls that big teacher/authority crap on us. This is my fourth year in debate, so I know Mr. Rogers pretty well.

Another thing I like about debate class is it's a miniature United Nations. There are Chinese, Japanese, Vietnamese, Filipino, Latino (Christy insists on Latina), black, white, even a girl who is part Cherokee. I guess this mix is true for a lot of my other classes, too. The difference in debate though is that we all talk to each other, we don't just stay in our own little look-alike groups.

Jeremy and I are both nationally recognized debaters. Several other Hamilton students are, too. Christy probably will have enough points for that next year, at the rate she's been going. She's usually shy in a group, or at a party. But when she stands in front of the class, or in front of a bunch of people at a debate tournament, she's awesome. She can be anything—brazen or meek, beautiful or ugly—whatever her character demands.

In the beginning no one paid much attention to Christy in this class, because she was so quiet I guess. But the first time she read from *The Color Purple* for Dramatic Interpretation, things changed. We'd been hanging around together for almost a month, and, although her reading impressed the whole class, it impressed me more.

She'd stood in front of the class, reading about how this woman loved a man, bodily. Her green, shining eyes met mine each time she glanced up from the book. I knew she'd chosen those pages for me. I still remember some of what it said: "I love his walk, his size, his shape, his smell . . ." She read on and on about the love of this woman for a man. And when she said the words, she looked like she was totally in love. No one talked, or even moved while she did her reading, and they stayed quiet for a while after. Then the whole class broke into applause.

"Wonderful!" Mr. Rogers said. "Excellent communication of feeling! Any suggestions for improvement? Is it a smooth cut?"

Everyone told her how good it was, no complaints. From that day on I had to get there early if I wanted to sit next to her. But that was okay. I knew who she'd been reading to, and it wasn't them. It was me.

And I also knew something else from that reading. I knew it was time to buy condoms, because I was sure it wouldn't be long before we did what I'd been wanting to do with her ever since our first kiss. That day, when she read from *The Color Purple*, my hopes weren't all that was high. I walked out of class carrying my notebook in front of me, hiding my anticipation.

But back to today. I'm already sitting in debate, in my usual place, when Christina and Kim walk right past me like I'm invisible and take seats on the opposite side of the room. I know I said I wished I'd never met Christy, but I did expect her to sit next to me like always. I mean, I don't understand why she won't even talk to me. So I get up and go sit beside her and ask, "How's it going?" but before the words are even out of my mouth, she picks up her books and walks back to the other side of the room. Kim follows her.

Practically the whole class notices.

"Oooohhh," they say in unison, almost like they'd practiced.

I feel my face burning and I know I'm turning red. I open my notebook and look down, like I'm studying something, but really I'm thinking, what's with her anyway? And Kim? What did I ever do to Kim? And the whole thing is seriously embarrassing.

Jeremy gets up from where he's sitting, next to where I *usually* sit when I'm not making a fool of myself trying to talk to Christina, and he comes over and sits by me.

Jeremy leans toward me and whispers, "Lover's spat, my man?"

Jeremy's word choices usually make me laugh. He likes to talk like he's somebody's grandfather. Today I am not amused.

I just shake my head no, keeping my eyes on the notebook in front of me. There's a lot of activity, people paired up, practicing speeches, checking reference materials, practicing Dramatic Interpretations. But I couldn't care less.

On the wall, over the jammed-full trophy case, there is a poster that says, "It is better to debate a question and leave it unresolved, than to resolve a question without debating it." That's one of the things I've learned in this class, to look at a question from all sides, to talk stuff through before reaching decisions. It worked for me on the curfew thing.

For a long time my mom insisted that I be home no later than one, even on weekends. I hated it. Most of my friends didn't have *any* curfews and nobody had to be in as early as I did. It was a joke. When I'd leave a party that was still going strong, Jeremy and Benny would yell out, "There goes J.B., working on his curfew merit badge."

Finally, after a lot of debating the question and leaving it unresolved, like the poster says, we agreed on two as a curfew. Mom thought that was too late, and I didn't want any curfew at all, but we reached a good compromise. She told me I should be a union negotiator instead of a teacher, but I don't think so. Anyway, no matter how much I wish Christy and the whole pregnancy issue would magically disappear, I know I've got to try to figure some things out with her.

After class, I catch up with her in the hall.

"We've got to talk," I say.

She keeps walking. I grab her arm.

"I mean it, Christy. I want to know what's going on."

"I already told you!" she says.

"Yeah, but I want to know more."

"There's no more to tell."

"Yes, there is. Meet me at my car after school."

She shakes her head no.

"Please, Christy. Please. We really do have to talk."

Finally she nods yes, and I go on to class. I don't know if she'll show up after school or not, but she does. We drive to the place by Safeway, where we'd parked after school in the days before I could actually take her home.

Christy's mom and dad are very strict, and her dad didn't want her dating, ever, under any circumstances. He's from Mexico and I guess they do things differently down there. For a long time Mr. Calderon wouldn't "allow" Christy to see me. But he couldn't keep us apart. In fact, maybe it made being together more exciting. One day though, I was so tired of sneaking around, I went to their house and I asked him to give me a chance. I told him we were going to see each other anyway.

It was scary. He's not a big guy, but he's muscular and he could probably throw a mean punch if he decided to. He got all red in the face and told me to leave. I did, but then the next night they invited me to their house for dinner, and her parents have liked me ever since. That would change fast if they knew the subject of our conversation right now.

"Are you sure you're pregnant?" I ask.

Christy looks at me like I'm an idiot.

"I haven't had a period since October first, I did a home pregnancy test that turned out positive, and the clinic test turned out positive. Half the time I throw up my breakfast, and look . . ."

She pulls her shirt way up. "Don't tell me you haven't noticed that I'm not flat chested anymore."

I'd never thought of her as flat chested. She was the one who used to always make jokes about it. To tell the truth I *had* noticed that she was getting bigger on top, but I thought maybe she was still developing. She's sixteen. That's possible, isn't it?

I pull her shirt back down. "Okay, okay," I say.

"Okay, what?"

"Okay, I guess you're pregnant."

"Don't guess, Jeff. It's true! I'm in my seventeenth week."

"I think it's not too late for an abortion," I say.

"I will *not* have an abortion! It's my body and it's my choice, and I choose NO ABORTION!"

"What are my choices?" I ask.

"That's your problem," she says.

"Christy . . ." I start, but don't know what to say. Finally I say, "I don't know how this happened."

"It happened with you having a good time."

"No, but you've been on the pill! You showed me your pills, in that little round container. I don't get it."

She looks away.

I see that she's crying, but don't rush to comfort her, like I used to. We sit for what seems like a long time.

"I need to go to work," I say.

"I know you don't love me anymore," she says, turning her face toward me, showing her tears. I say nothing.

"Even if you don't love me, we have a responsibility to our baby," she says.

"We have a responsibility to ourselves," I say, "to give us a chance in life first, before we mess up some poor kid."

"I thought I could always depend on you, that you'd always be there for me," she says, sobbing and catching her breath.

"I thought I could depend on you, too. When you said you couldn't get pregnant, I believed you. Now look at the mess we're in."

She just sits there, crying. I fish around in the glove compartment for a tissue and hand it to her, then start the car and drive her home.

After work I sit at the desk in my room, with the door closed. I list the pros and cons of Christy getting an abortion. Maybe if I show it to her she will reconsider. I write:

Reasons not to have an abortion:

It will hurt.

Maybe it's a sin.

Reasons to have an abortion:

Having a baby will hurt a lot more.

It's not murder! It doesn't have a brain yet—it's a mass of cells, that's all.

It's too soon to have a baby because you and I both have to finish school.

We couldn't be free. We're too young to be tied down.

It would really upset our parents if they knew you were pregnant.

Why should we pay for the rest of our lives for some stupid mix-up with birth control pills?

Christy—worst of all, the world is probably going to be an awful place to live in by the time the baby would even get to high school. The whole ocean is polluted and there won't be enough food to go around. The air will be unbreathable. Think about the poor, innocent life without a chance of happiness.

When I read the list over, I don't see how Christy can even consider going through with this pregnancy. It was a stupid mistake that needs to be corrected as soon as possible.

Tuesday morning I put the list in an envelope and seal it. On the front, in big black letters, I write CHRISTY— PLEASE THINK ABOUT THIS. Even though it means I'll be late to my first class, I walk across campus to where I know Christy's English class is, and I give her the envelope.

"See me at the car after school?" I ask.

"Okay," she says, and she smiles her old smile at me. I think everything's going to work out.

After school I wait and wait, but Christy doesn't show up. I drive past her house and also past Kim's house. She's not at either place. I go to work, determined to put the whole thing out of my mind until tomorrow. Instead I end up doing a mental review of our history together, trying to figure out how things managed to go from being so great to being so messed up.

4

When Christy and I first got together everything was going good for me. Like I already said, it was the beginning of my junior year at Hamilton High School. I'd been working at the Fitness Club, getting in a few sets on the machines most days. I got a car, an '88 Jetta. I bought it from my Uncle Steve, and he gave me a really good deal on it. It wasn't the car of my dreams, but it was all mine. No more begging rides from friends, or waiting for my mom to come pick me up like I was some little Cub Scout.

Okay. I was feeling good about my car, and also I'd gotten kind of buff—built some bulk and definition. I know it sounds conceited, but I'm trying to be totally honest, so I admit it. I liked my body. Not that I was like those body builders you see in magazines, all greased up, with veins roadmapped over giant muscles and with necks the size of my thigh. There are some guys at the club like that and to tell the truth they gross me out. I'm not that extreme.

Just before school started that year, when I got home from my annual summer visit to my grandma in Florida, my mom told me I looked like a bronze god. But that's just my mom. I wouldn't go that far.

So where are we here? I was a junior, with a car and a

pretty good body—a few very important things along the road to manhood. Oh, yeah. And I'd gotten my braces off in August, just before I went to Florida. That may not sound like a big deal, but believe me, if you've been wearing braces for most of your adolescent life, it *is* a very big deal to see your teeth again, and to be able to eat popcorn, and to smile without sticking your hand in front of your mouth.

Anyway, it was at that debate party at Dashan's, September 17, that things got started between me and Christina. It's funny. I can close my eyes and remember exactly how it was that night.

"How do you like Hamilton High?" I'd asked her. (I'm not a great conversationalist.)

"I like it," she said, "but I miss my old friends."

"Where did you go before?"

"St. Catherine's."

"Really?" I'd said, laughing.

"What's funny?"

"I don't know. I've never talked to a girl from that school. Aren't they really strict, and religious?"

"No. Well . . . more than here. My dad wanted me to go to Mission High after St. Catherine's, but I finally talked him into letting me come to Hamilton. My mom helped."

She told me she wanted to come to Hamilton because Mission didn't offer sign language as a foreign language. Also because of Hamilton's program for the hearing impaired. She wanted to be an aide in those classes. She was only in the ninth grade, and she already knew she wanted a career working with deaf kids. She got interested in that kind of work when she was only ten years old and a three-year-old deaf girl moved in next door to them.

"It was so sad," she'd told me. "That little girl, Sarah, had to work so hard to communicate—and I saw that I could help. I understood her better than her mother did. I don't exactly know why, but it's like a special intuition.

Sarah was already learning to sign, and I learned some with her. But I want to get better at it."

From the very beginning, I liked that Christy cared about people. Later, when I got to know her family, I saw that her mother was like that, too. Mrs. Calderon was always fixing food for a family where the mom was sick, or listening on the phone to someone else's problems. As far as I could tell, Mr. Calderon mostly cared about being the big boss. But once he helped me replace some hoses on my car. I know he's not all bad, he's just often very difficult to get along with. Mrs. Calderon, though—she's always nice.

But back to the party where Christy and I first talked. We danced for a while, and talked. It was hot and loud in the house, so we went for a walk. There was a cool, light breeze and the air smelled almost clean. I remember how good it felt to be outside, walking along next to Christina.

"Look. See that big house behind those trees?" I asked, pointing in the direction of a huge, run-down house at the end of the street.

"Jeremy and I used to think it was haunted. Jeremy lives just around the corner, and we used to sneak down here at night when I'd stay at his house. We wanted to see a ghost."

"Do you believe in ghosts?" she asked.

"Not anymore, but I did when I was little. Once Jeremy and I opened a door to a shed. Look. If you look right through there you can see it."

I stood behind Christina and put my hands on her head, turning it gently to the angle where I thought she could see the old shed. Her hair was soft and fine feeling. She smelled clean and soapy. I leaned closer to her.

"I see it," she said. "What happened when you opened the door?"

"What?" I'd lost track of our conversation, wondering whether or not I should try to kiss her.

"Your story, about ghosts," she said, turning to me and smiling a half-smile, like maybe she'd read my mind.

"What happened when you opened the shed door?"

I could feel my face warming and I knew I was turning red. Thank God it was dark.

"Well, when we pushed the door open, we heard this thud, and then a loud, frantic, flapping sound. We ran like crazy and didn't stop 'til we got back to Jeremy's."

"What caused the noise?"

"We had it all figured out. According to our theory, a body made the heavy thudding sound, and when the body fell, that loosened the ghost inside it—which was what all the flapping was about." I laughed. "We were ten. What can I say?"

"I believe in ghosts," Christina said.

"You do?"

"Yes. I believe every soul lives forever, and that people who have bad things happen to them in their lives keep hovering around as ghosts, and if you've done something bad to someone you might end up being haunted by that person."

Thinking about that conversation now, I suddenly realize that if Christy thinks this mass of cells she's calling a baby is going to turn into a ghost and haunt her forever, she'll never go through with an abortion. I hope she's outgrown all that ghost stuff by now, but I doubt it. She'd been very definite about her belief in ghosts that night.

"I don't believe in ghosts at all anymore," I'd told her.

"Well, how about the ghost you and Jeremy found in the shed?"

"It was no ghost, it was our imagination. We probably just knocked over a big bag of fertilizer—that was the thud. And it startled some birds that were nesting in there. Want to go see?" I asked, taking her hand and pulling her in that direction.

"No!" she screamed.

"Okay, okay. I was only kidding," I said.

"Don't kid about ghosts!"

I could see that she was truly frightened. I put my arm

around her and she didn't move away. In fact, she even leaned toward me. We walked back to the party, close, and got a soda.

"Did Dashan ever sneak around that place with you and Jeremy?"

"No. Dashan never did anything to get in trouble, even then. He was born good . . . See?" I said, pointing to where Dashan was dancing with his eight-year-old sister, Takasha, making her laugh.

"I know, he's really nice. Besides you, he's the only guy in debate who talks to me. At first I thought . . . well . . . you know, a black guy . . . I've never talked to a black guy before, but now I really like him."

"You mean there weren't any black kids at St. Catherine's?"

"Nope. Just us Mexicans and you white guys," she said, laughing.

"No Asians?" I asked.

"Hardly any," she said.

"How boring," I said, thinking that debate wouldn't be nearly as much fun if we were missing the black kids, like Dashan and Michelle, and the Asian kids, like Trin and Hung. When it was time for me to go I told Christy, "I'd like to take you home, but I'm walking. I've got to wait until payday to put gas in my car."

"It's okay. My mom and dad are coming to pick me and Kim up any minute now. My dad won't let me go out unless he drives me to and from wherever I'm going. It's kind of embarrassing."

"At least he cares," I said, thinking about how long it had been since I'd been anywhere with my dad. "Can I call you tomorrow?"

She hesitated, then gave me her phone number, which I stuffed way down in my back pocket so I'd be sure not to lose it.

"Walk out with me," I said.

We walked together to the end of Dashan's driveway. I

gave her a quick kiss. She smiled. I loved that smile.

"'Night, Jeff," she said. I liked how she said my name. I liked how she looked, how she smelled, the way she danced, the way she looked straight into my eyes when I talked to her, everything. I liked everything about her. Even now I can remember how I felt that night, seventeen months ago.

My mom was still up when I got home from the party, stretched out on the couch, watching the end of some old Spencer Tracy, Katherine Hepburn movie. Books and papers were strewn all over the coffee table—physiology, chemistry. She glanced at the clock and, I guess, decided not to hassle me for being twenty minutes late.

"Want some hot chocolate?" she said, getting up. "I'm fixing some for me."

"No, thanks."

"How was the party?"

"Fine."

"Tell me about it."

"It was just a party," I said.

I followed her into the kitchen and sat at the table, watching her stir powdered chocolate mix into the pan of milk that was warming on the stove. She put two cups of hot chocolate on the table.

"I don't want any, Mom."

"Come on, it will help you sleep."

"I don't have trouble sleeping. You're the one who has trouble sleeping, not me."

"I don't have trouble sleeping," she said.

"Why aren't you asleep now?"

"Because I can't sleep until you get home. You know that."

"Then you have trouble sleeping."

"No. You have trouble getting home."

"Mom . . ."

"I worry. That's all. Not about what you'll do. I trust you. I know you're sensible, and a good person. But it's everyone else . . . Did you see on TV last night, not more than three miles from here a boy was gunned down right in front of his house?"

"That's different, Mom. I'm not in a gang. That's stupid gang stuff."

"It's not only gang kids that get shot. You know that."

"Don't start, Ma. You can't always be worrying about me. I'm okay."

"I know," she sighed. "I just can't help it."

We sat silently, sipping our hot chocolate, which tasted pretty good after all.

After a while I told her, "I met a girl tonight."

My mom put down her cup and gave me one of those intense stares, like already she knew something I didn't know.

"Tell me about her."

"She's only fourteen . . ."

"To your ancient sixteen," my mom said.

"She's nice, though."

"You must have some feeling that she's kind of special."

"Nah. She's just a girl," I said, rinsing my cup and putting it in the dishwasher. "See you in the morning," I said.

That night I'd climbed into bed and thought about Christina—her silky hair, her fresh smell, how soft she felt leaning toward me when I put my arm around her. Why hadn't I tried to kiss her for real, not just that little, quick kiss? Why hadn't I tried to hold her close to me? I could imagine how it would feel to have my arms around her, my mouth on her soft lips, her body close, close to mine.

I was always telling myself I wouldn't do that stuff again, but I admit, I used my hand to make me feel good while I thought about Christina. I was quiet, and careful about the sheets, but if I hadn't done that, I think I'd have been awake all night long.

Even though Steve had told me a long time ago, like

when I was eleven and we had our sex talk, that mastur-
bation was a perfectly natural thing, I couldn't help feeling
guilty.

Benny's older brother warned us once that if we were
always getting ourselves off we'd get too much in the habit
of hurrying. He said girls don't like guys who are too quick
on the trigger. I hoped I wasn't some kind of pervert, or
ruining myself for girls, but sometimes a guy's just got to
give in. That's what I thought, and it's part of my honest
story.

Anyway, since that night at Dashan's party, Christy and
I have been together. And in spite of all I've been saying,
like how I'm trying to break up with her and I wish we'd
never met, for a long time I thought she was the best thing
to ever come my way, and I wanted to be around her all the
time.

That first semester we didn't have the same lunch
period, so sometimes I would take my lunch into the
classroom where she was an aide. The teacher always had
a hard time with this one kid, Max. He'd run around the
classroom, throwing stuff at the other kids. But Christy
could put her hands on his shoulders and he'd immediately
give her his attention. They would "talk" in sign language,
and then he'd sit at his desk and get to work. I was
impressed that she had such rapport with Max when the
professional teacher couldn't even reach that kid. The
teacher was impressed, too.

But even though Christy was very talented in debate,
and did a great job as an aide in the Hearing Impaired
program, her dad treated her like she was a troublemaker.
I guess he was just protective, but sometimes he was
totally unreasonable. Like the first time she was scheduled
to compete in an out-of-town debate tournament, he told
her she couldn't go. The whole team was depending on her,
but he accused her of lying and said there *was* no tourna-

ment, it was just an excuse for her to be out running around.

When Mr. Rogers finally convinced Mr. Calderon that there really was an out-of-town tournament, he said it didn't matter, girls shouldn't be doing that kind of thing anyway. Although he gave in at the last minute, he put Christy through hell for days before he changed his mind.

Sometimes Christy got so angry that she would leave the house, determined not to go back. Then I'd find her waiting for me after work. I'd hold her tight while she cried out her frustration. Then I'd take her home with me and my mom would talk with us both, saying if Christy needed an emergency place to stay she could stay with us for a day or two, but we'd have to call her house to say she was okay. Then Mrs. Calderon would answer the phone, crying, begging Christy to come home.

By that time she would have managed to get Mr. Calderon calmed down, and I'd end up taking Christy home. Then her dad would give in on whatever they had been arguing about and everything would be okay until the next big blow-up.

"I wish things were as easy-going at my house as they are at yours," Christy often said. And she also often said she didn't know what she would do without me—that I was the only one who had ever really truly cared about her. I don't know why Christy thought her mom didn't care. It seemed to me that her mom cared a lot, but Christy didn't think so.

"She *always* takes my dad's side, no matter how stupid he's being."

"She only does that to get around him," I'd tell her.

"But you're the only one I can depend on in my whole life," she would say.

Anyway, I felt important, and needed, and for the first year or so I liked that feeling.

Another thing, in the beginning, Christy and I used to laugh all the time. She could mimic all of the teachers and she had a way of doing the unexpected that cracked me up. It was never mean or anything, just funny.

Also, I liked having sex with her, too. I really, really, liked that part. Just thinking about it now gets me all horny. That's a problem I have.

I gather dirty towels around the gym floor and dump them into the hamper and put the weights back in their proper places in the racks, getting ready to sign out for the evening. All of this looking back on my seventeen months with Christy reminds me that even though I want to break up with her now, I'll never forget the good times we've had together.

After work I drive past her house. I really need to talk with her. No one is home.

CHAPTER

5

Mom left a note on the refrigerator for me. "Gone shopping with May—I'll be back by eight with pizza." I hope she brings back pepperoni and not that cheeseless vegetarian stuff she gets sometimes when she's on a health kick.

I bring my books to the kitchen table and start working on my D.I. piece for the March tournament. If my personal life weren't so screwed up right now I'd be excited about the March trip. We're going to San Diego and we'll be competing with kids from all over the state. Whoever qualifies in San Diego will go on to the national competition in New Orleans. I barely missed nationals last year, and I really want to make it this year. It's my last chance. I think I can do it.

I'm trying to decide between two possibilities. One is from a play called "Sex, Drugs, Rock & Roll" by this guy Eric Bogosian. He writes about real life stuff, which I like. I may do something from his play about a homeless man who's always trying to be positive even though his total food intake is only one egg sandwich a day.

The other thing I like is from a short story. I have to decide. The short story, by Ethan Canin, is about a time in a sixteen-year-old kid's life when his mom has decided he and his dad should get to know each other better. So, at the mom's insistence, the kid hides in the trunk of his dad's car to see where he goes when he takes Sunday drives.

It ends up that the dad goes to meet a woman and they have wild sex in the back seat of the car, while this kid is just on the other side of the seat, in the trunk, getting all jostled around. It's funny and sad all at the same time. It's hard to choose. The one about the homeless guy gets more emotional, and that's good for a D.I.—adds interest. On the other hand, it's fairly common for debaters to use things from Eric Bogosian. Hardly anyone has even heard of this Ethan Canin guy, in debate anyway. It's a definite advantage to be using fresh material.

There's a part in the Canin story I hate, though. On a trip, again arranged by the mom, the dad tells the kid, "You don't have to get to know me, because one day you're going to grow up, and then you're going to *be* me." I'm not going to include that part. Guys don't always turn out to be exact replicas of their dads. I know *I* won't. I'll probably do the thing about the homeless guy, anyway. Right now I don't want to think about sex at all, even if there's humor in it.

When I told Mr. Rogers I was having a hard time deciding between the two pieces, he gave me the advice he always gives. Look for something that touches you, he always says. You must have passion for your script. I guess the script I have the most passion for is that father/son thing. I'm always trying to fill in the blanks in my own life that have been left by my father's absence. I feel very strongly about that topic. Okay, so I guess I've made my decision. Now all I have to do is decide how to tie everything together in a script.

Mom walks into the kitchen carrying a giant pizza box with a new crossword puzzle book on top. Before she went back to school she used to always be doing crossword puzzles. Now, because she has to study so much, she limits herself to one a week.

"Dinner!" she yells.

"It's about time. I'm starving!"

I open the box to be sure it's the good kind, but I can already smell the pepperoni so I know I'll like it. I get out cold sodas while Mom makes a salad. I'm on my second piece of pizza when there's a knock at the back door.

"Anybody home?"

It's Stacy. She can pick up the scent of pizza from inside her house, across the street from us, even if the doors and windows are shut tight and the air conditioner is on full blast.

"Help yourself, Stacy," Mom says, laughing.

Stacy gets a plate and a soda and sits down next to me. She eyes the pizza, then takes the biggest piece.

"Jeez, Stacy! Butt in on our pizza parade and then take the piece that clearly had my name on it!" I punch her, lightly, on the arm.

"I'm saving you from a life of obesity," she says, taking a giant bite of the thin-crusted, double cheese and pepperoni delicacy. Stacy is almost as tall as I am, and really, really skinny, but she eats more than anyone I know.

"Hey, did you read the history assignment for tomorrow?" she asks.

"Yeah."

"What was it about?"

"The Civil War," I say.

"I know that much. Be specific."

"Go read your own chapter, you bum," I say, reaching past her for another piece of pizza.

"I don't know how you can stand him, Mommy Karen," Stacy says, using her long-time pet name for my mom.

"He grows on you. Give him time."

Stacy and I have been pretending not to like each other since she moved in across the street when we were both in the second grade. In some ways, though, we're like best friends, or maybe like brother and sister. Neither of us would know about that brother/sister stuff because neither of us has one. Well, my dad has another son, I think he's about eight or so, and biologically speaking, I guess he's my half-brother. But I've only seen him about four times in my whole life, so I don't think he counts. Whatever. Stacy and I spent a lot of time at each other's houses when we were growing up. She liked my mom better than her own, and I liked to watch her dad work around their house, just to get an idea of what dads could do.

We played army and cop stuff, and we climbed trees and built forts. Stacy was a tomboy, so it worked out fine. When we got a little older we played gin rummy about six hours a day. That was back before either of us had a job.

Stacy works for a veterinarian down by school. That's what she says she wants to be, but her grades are from hell.

"Okay. I got the dinner, you guys clean up," Mom says, taking her crossword puzzle book and heading for her favorite chair in the den.

Stacy rinses while I load the dishwasher. I put the leftover pizza in the fridge, she wipes the table. Just as we finish cleaning up, the phone rings.

"Hello?" I say.

It is Christy. "No abortions," she says, then hangs up.

I put the phone back on the receiver and give the table another swipe with the dishcloth.

"Who was that?" Mom yells from the den.

"Wrong number," I say.

"Wanna shoot a few baskets?" Stacy asks.

"Sure." That's one thing Stacy got by having a dad—a basketball hoop with lights bright enough we can play all night unless the neighbors complain.

"Hey, Mom, I'm goin' to Stacy's for a little while," I say.

"Wait! Four letters. Roman poet. Blank, 'v,' blank, blank," Mom yells from the den.

"Ovid," I yell back.

"Thanks! See ya later."

Stacy gives me a disgusted look. "How do you know that stuff, anyway?"

"I go to my classes. I don't sit doing kissy-kissy things in my car in the school parking lot like you and Frankie-boy do."

Stacy punches me in the arm, hard. "Nosy."

I punch her back. "Indiscreet."

"What's *that* supposed to mean?"

"Look it up," I say, laughing.

She stands, eyebrows raised, her kinky blond hair sticking out all over her head. I think she's going to punch me again, but instead she says, "It sounds like you and Christy have been doing a lot more than kissy-kissy."

"What do you mean?"

"Well, you know. Word gets around," she says.

"Word? What word?"

"Oh, aren't you Mr. Innocent," she says, then she starts singing, "Lullaby and goodnight, da da da da and sleep tight . . ."

I grab her by the arm. "What the hell are you talking about?"

She laughs.

"Get serious!"

Her smile fades and she gives me this long look.

"Okay. I heard something at school today that surprised me."

"Tell me."

"It was in gym. My locker's right next to Kim's and she and Christy were standing there having a very serious conversation. I don't think they even noticed me. I didn't mean to eavesdrop but, you know . . ."

"So?"

"So Kim was saying she was sure you'd come around. Her cousin or somebody was really upset when his girl-friend told him she was pregnant, and then pretty soon he was always wanting to feel the baby kick, and making her eat vegetables and drink milk," Stacy says. "And then Kim goes 'it was so purty,' in that little-girl voice that makes me want to barf."

I groan.

"So how about it, Jeffie—gonna be a dad?"

"I don't know. I don't want to. Don't say anything about this to anyone, okay, Stace?"

"Hey, my lips are sealed. But face it, if Kim knows, the whole school will probably know by Friday."

I sit down on the curb and stare into the gutter.

"So it's true?"

Stacy sits beside me, and I tell her the whole story. In a way it helps to talk about it, but in another way it makes the whole thing seem more real.

"What can I do, Stace?" I ask. "I'm set to start college in September. I can't have a kid now."

"Do you think Christy might change her mind about an abortion?"

"I doubt it," I sigh.

"Sounds like you're going to be a dad, whether you like it or not."

"But it's not fair!"

"Well, I hate to say it, old pal, but you play, you pay—your mom's gonna be super upset."

"I hope she never finds out. I keep hoping *something* will happen, that it's all a bad dream, or Christy will start her period, or *something*!"

It's after ten when I hear a car pull into our driveway.

Mom pulls back the curtain in the dining room and looks out.

"Who is it?" I ask.

"Well, it's Christy and her father. I wonder what they could want at this time of night. I hope they're not fighting again."

I want to run out the back door, down the street, just keep running until I find a place where no one knows me.

Run to Canada, or Alaska. My legs are tense with wanting to run. But instead, I stand, paralyzed, rooted in place, with sweating palms and quickened breath.

Mom goes to the door and opens it, smiling.

"Come in, Christina, Mr. Calderon. What brings you out tonight?"

Mr. Calderon pushes Christy in ahead of him. I can see that she has been crying. She doesn't look at me.

"Look at this, Mrs. Browning. Look at what your son has done!"

Christy's dad is waving a paper in my mom's face. My chest tightens around my pounding heart. It's the note I gave Christy this morning, the one listing all the reasons she should have an abortion.

"Perhaps we could sit down and talk, Mr. Calderon," Mom says, backing away from him and sitting on the hard pine bench next to the fireplace, leaving the comfortable overstuffed sofa for Christy and her dad.

"Look at this! You look at this! Then say sit down or not!"

My mom takes the note from him, and I lean my head against the cool wall, trying to slow the swirling in my brain.

"Jeffrey!" Mom says. "What does this mean?"

I can't look at her. I keep my head against the wall.

"Jeffrey!"

I turn. The color is drained from her face. Christy's face is swollen with crying. Mr. Calderon's face is dark with rage.

"Explain this, Jeff," my mom says, her eyes wide, waiting.

"He's made my daughter pregnant, and now he wants to kill."

"Jeff?" my mom says, not taking her eyes from me.

"I don't know, Mom. Christy says she's pregnant."

"He forced her! Christina is a good girl!" Christy's dad is yelling, stomping. It's worse than an earthquake. Mom looks away from me to him.

"SHUT UP!"

Her scream is so loud, so piercing, that everything stops. Then, in a quiet voice, almost a whisper, she says, "Come sit down, Jeff." She pats the bench beside her, as if she were inviting a nine-year-old me to hear a bedtime story. I take my place beside her.

"Tell me, is Christy pregnant?"

Mr. Calderon pulls another piece of paper from his shirt pocket and shoves it in my mother's hand.

"My wife found this. She is home now, crying her eyes out over our little girl."

He paces back and forth in front of the windows, watching as Mom reads the clinic results. Christy has her head down, hands over her face.

"Well. I guess she *is* pregnant," Mom says, holding the paper toward me. I don't reach for it.

"I've seen it."

"I suppose so," she says softly, crumpling it in her hand.

"Mr. Calderon, please sit down and stop pacing," Mom says. "You're making me very nervous."

"Nervous! Nervous is nothing, Mrs. Browning. Having your daughter pregnant from a bad boy, that is something! Nervous is nothing!"

"Daddy, please," Christy says.

"He will marry her! There will be a wedding!"

"Mr. Calderon, Christy, I need to talk to Jeff alone. Please leave us alone."

"I don't leave until I have his word on marriage," he says, standing over Mom, looking down on her like one of those gargoyles they have on old buildings.

"You leave or I call the cops!" she says, getting up and standing to face him. "Leave now!"

He looks at my mother, stunned. He's not used to having a woman stand up to him. He takes two long strides to where Christy is sitting, grabs her by the wrist and pulls her to the door. She doesn't look back. Mom closes the door behind them, then sinks onto the sofa.

"God, Jeff, how could you have let this happen? I thought I'd raised you to be so responsible. You've always seemed to have such a good head on your shoulders."

She sits, tears streaming down her face, looking at me as if I'm a stranger. "It's not that you didn't know better. God," she sighs, never taking her eyes from my face. She reads the pregnancy test results again, shaking her head.

I don't know what to say. When I was thirteen my mom enrolled me in a human sexuality course at Planned Parenthood. She told me she wished it was like the old days, when people took sex seriously and waited until they were married to do it, but she knew things had changed, and she wanted me to be fully informed, so I wouldn't get myself in any messes—like, with disease, or pregnancy. She talked to me about sex, and respecting myself and others, being careful. So did Uncle Steve. What she says is true. I knew better.

I try to explain my side of things. "It wasn't all my fault, Mom. She was on the pill. She even showed me."

"Oh, Jesus! What were you thinking with? Your penis?"

I pick up the letter I had given Christy earlier in the day.

"But see, Mom, don't you think it makes sense for her to get an abortion?"

"Yes. It makes sense to me. It makes sense to you. Maybe it would make sense to most people. But if it doesn't make sense to Christy, forget it. It's her decision. And I don't think Christy is going to run to the nearest abortion clinic."

"What do you think, Mom? What should I do?"

She looks at me, hard. "It doesn't seem to matter what I think. It didn't matter that I told you never to have sex without a condom, no matter what, and nothing I think or say matters now. You've made one huge, foolish, life-changing mistake. I am disappointed in you beyond words." She pauses, wiping her teary eyes. "All of those years of your grandma and I cutting corners, trying to save money so you could go to college—did you think that was easy? She and I may as well cash in the savings and go to England because you sure as hell aren't going away to college now."

Her words cut into me. I can't look at her. "I'm sorry, Mom," I say.

"It's not like spilling your milk, Jeff. Sorry doesn't help."

She gets up from the sofa and walks slowly down the hall to her bedroom, closing the door behind her. I go out to the den, turn on the TV and channel-surf about ten times around all of the stations. Nothing. Nothing will take me away from me. I step outside. It is cool, dark. I walk. Past the market, past the park, past my old elementary school. When I get to Steve's apartment building I stop and look up at his windows. Not a light on. What could he do for me anyway? What can anyone do, except Christy, and she won't do it. I walk on, fantasizing about some minor accident that would jar the fetus loose—nothing awful, just a natural abortion.

The noise of cars whizzing along on the freeway startles me. I must have been walking in some kind of daze. I've come a long way. I walk to the middle of the overpass and look down. It must be midnight by now. This freeway is never quiet. The L.A. Basin, home to the homeless. Home to smog, and earthquakes, and riots, and constant movement on jampacked freeways. For what? For what? I grip the chain link fence that is attached to the overpass and push forward as far as it will give.

"For what?" I scream down at the speeding cars.

I look up at the curved top of the fence. They fenced all the overpasses along about a ten mile segment of this freeway last year, after some tenth grader at Emerson High jumped off—bit the big one. It would be easy to get over the curve, though, if a person wanted to badly enough. I jump up, grasp the fence where it curves inward, and hang there for a moment. It would be easy to swing my feet to the lower part of the fence and grapple my way higher, to the top, and then shift my balance to the outside of the fence. Easy. Easy as pie.

I let go and drop to the sidewalk, watch the cars for a

while longer, then turn back in the direction of home. When I get there I see the kitchen light is on and my mom is sitting at the table, drinking tea. I walk past her but she calls me back. She stands up and puts her arms around me.

"I'm sorry, Jeffie," she says. "I said some mean things."

"I guess I deserve it."

"No, Sweetheart. We all make mistakes. I've made lots of mistakes. We live with them, we learn from them, and we go on. This is a tough one, but it's not like cancer, or being homeless, or not having a family that cares. And it's not like you're a mass murderer. I love you, mistakes and all."

She hugs me tighter and that does it. All of the worry and frustration I've been feeling breaks loose, and I start crying. And that gets my mom going, too. We stand with our arms around each other, both of us sobbing. I feel her warm tears against my shirt and look down on the top of her head. For the first time ever I get this feeling that she's sort of, I don't know how to explain it, breakable, maybe.

I'm sorry I've disappointed my mom. I'm sorry I got Christy pregnant, even if it was a lot her own fault. I'm sorry my life isn't going the way I thought it would. I'm even sorry for Mr. and Mrs. Calderon. But what my mom said earlier is true—sorry doesn't help. I wish it did.

6

When the alarm rings at six-thirty I turn over and go back to sleep. At least I try to go back to sleep. Then everything from the night before washes over me and I get that closed-in feeling again. There's a story about a fox who was caught in a steel trap and it gnawed its own foot off in order to get free. All that was left in the trap when the hunter checked was a severed, bloody paw. If only I could gnaw my way out of this trap I'm in right now, I think I'd do it.

"Aren't you going to school?" my mom says, peeking around my bedroom door.

"No. I feel awful," I say, which is the truth.

She comes in, sits on the edge of my bed, and feels my forehead. "No fever."

"I'm beat, Mom."

She nods as if she understands. I never miss school unless I'm on the critical list, but today I will. So what?

"What are your plans?" Mom asks.

"Just hang around here—probably go to work this afternoon."

"I don't mean *today*, Jeff. I mean plans like Christy/baby plans."

"I have no plans," I say.

"Do you think her dad is serious about expecting you to marry her?" She gives me a long, intense look.

"Probably, knowing him."

"What do you think about the marriage idea?" she says.

"I think it sucks."

We discuss what my mother refers to as my predicament. She says she'll stand by my decision not to marry Christy, no matter what Mr. Calderon says. Why be twice as idiotic as I've already been is how she puts it.

"But Jeff, you've got a responsibility to this life you've started."

"But I didn't *want* to start a new life."

She looks at me, like that's too stupid to even consider. I know what that look means—if I didn't want to start a new life, why didn't I take my own precautions?

"I want you to know I've done my childrearing stint, Jeff. If I had it to do over again, I'd do it the same way—marry the same jerk, just so I could get the same kid. But I'm on the verge of a new career, something I've wanted to do for years, and I'm not going to be one of those grandmothers who raises their kid's kid . . . Don't even think about it."

"God, Mom. I'm not thinking there's going to be *be* a kid."

"I think you're wrong about that. I think you're going to get a kid."

We talk for a long time. There aren't any easy answers, but I feel a little better anyway. Then my mom tells me she's going to call Christy's parents and invite them to come over tonight.

"God! Why?"

"Because I told Mr. Calderon to come back tonight. Because we're all involved in this, one way or another."

I take a shower while she's on the phone so I don't have to hear even one side of the conversation. I dread the evening.

Ever since I got to know her, Christy's mom liked me a lot. Whenever I'd go over there she'd give me a big hug and a kiss on the cheek. She always called me *mi hijo*, meaning son, and she felt kind of like a second mom to me, too. She always had something for me to eat, even if I'd stopped by just for a minute.

In my house, my mom and I each take care of our own stuff. Sometimes we eat together and sometimes we don't. She's raised me to be self-sufficient—fix a basic meal, clean up after myself, do my own laundry, that kind of thing. But Mrs. Calderon would always wait on me. I admit I liked it.

When the Calderons arrive at our house this evening, though, there is no kissing, or calling me *mi hijo*. Neither of Christy's parents will so much as look at me. Christy ignores me, too. All three of them say hello to my mom, but I guess I'm invisible.

Mr. Calderon is wearing a tie and Mrs. Calderon is wearing high heeled shoes and the pearls she wears every Sunday. They seem formal—stiff. Christy is wearing jeans and a big sweatshirt that comes down to her thighs. No one is smiling.

My mom offers coffee or tea to everyone, like this is going to be a party. I think we should get it over with, not waste our time making a social event of it.

Mr. and Mrs. Calderon both say they'd like a cup of coffee, then Christy asks, "Do you have anything without caffeine, Mrs. Browning?"

What's with her? She drinks coffee by the gallon. I've never seen anyone drink coffee the way Christy does. Except, now that I think of it, I haven't seen Christy drink coffee lately. Also, it's been a while since I've seen her wearing anything but jeans and a long sweatshirt.

"I've got some herbal tea," Mom says. "Would you like that?"

"Please," she says.

I follow Mom out to the kitchen and help bring out the drinks. No way am I going to sit in the living room, alone with the Calderons.

The first thing Christy's dad says after he gets his coffee and one of those little chocolate-covered Pogen cookies is that Christy and I have to get married right away.

I say I'm not ready to get married yet. Mr. Calderon starts that pacing business again, like he was doing last night. Mrs. Calderon starts crying, and Christy sits still as a statue, her face turned away from me. No one says anything. The only sound is of Mr. Calderon's footsteps, softened by the carpet, and the ticking of the clock. The question I asked myself standing on the freeway bridge comes back to me. What am I doing here? Tick. Tick. Tick. Then, after about his tenth trip, back and forth, back and forth, in rhythm with the clock, he explodes.

"I KNEW IT!" he yells. "I KNEW IT! I KNEW IT! I KNEW IT!" He is facing his wife, who sits covering her face with her hands, shaking with silent sobs. "She should have stayed with the nuns at the mission! Never ever should she have met this bad boy! She was a good girl and now she is ruined. He has taken my daughter and turned her to dirt!"

"Mr. Calderon . . ." my mom starts.

"This boy! This big-shot, debate team, going-to-college boy has ruined her! He is not ready to marry! Not ready! Not ready? Ready to make babies! Ready to turn girls to dirt!"

He stomps over and stands directly in front of me, looking down at me, pointing his finger.

"You will marry Christina!"

"Daddy!" Christina yells. She is on her feet and standing between us, nose to nose with her father.

"I will not marry anyone who doesn't love me! Who doesn't want to marry me! You can't make me!"

I'm shocked. I've never, ever seen her talk back to her father.

She turns on me. "I wouldn't have you, you . . . you . . . baby killer!" She is screaming, red faced.

"Calm down," I say to Christy, but she's already turned

back to her dad.

"You! All you care about is what your stupid old church says!"

He gasps. Then yells, "Sacrilege! You are not my daughter!" He slaps her, hard. "Tramp!"

I jump between them, standing so close I can feel his breath in my face. My fists are clenched tight. My mom rushes in.

"Stop this instant!" she says, pushing Mr. Calderon toward the other side of the room.

I feel Christy's head against my back, feel her shaking sobs. Her mother is up now, begging her father to sit down. I turn and put my arms around Christy. Her dad walks out the door, slamming it behind him, rattling the windows in the living room. A car door slams and Mr. Calderon drives away.

Christy steps away from me. We stand looking at each other, shocked into silence. Then my mom gets an ice pack for Christy. Her face is white with the imprint of her dad's four fingers.

"You stay here tonight," my mom says to Christy.

Christy shakes her head no. Her mom opens her arms to Christy and they stand in an embrace, rocking, both of them crying. After a while Mom says, "Has your father ever hit you before?"

Both Christy and her mom say he hasn't.

"Maybe a little spank," Christy says. "But he's never really hit me, like this."

"I think I should call the police and report this," my mom says. "It is child abuse, you know."

Mrs. Calderon pleads with my mom not to do that.

"He will be all right now. I know him. It is all right. He will be sorry."

The two moms and Christy talk about I don't know what. I can hardly listen. I keep thinking if only she'd agreed to an abortion, and not left her private papers sitting around—or, if only I'd always used a condom . . . or

. . . if only I'd broken up with Christy in the fall, when I knew it should be over . . . if only, if only, if only.

About forty-five minutes after Christy and her mom leave, there is a knock on the front door. My mom opens it a crack, then takes off the safety chain and opens it wide. I listen from the den.

"I guess I have to stay here tonight after all, Mrs. Browning," I hear Christy say. "My dad won't let me in. He says I don't live there anymore."

I hear Christy crying, and Mom murmuring something. After a while they come into the den.

"Jeff, get the sheets and a couple of blankets from the linen closet, would you, and help me make up this bed," Mom says, pointing to the sofa bed where I'm sitting.

"He wouldn't even let me take any clothes, or my books for school, or anything," Christy says.

My mom brings a flannel nightgown.

"Take a shower, Honey. You'll feel better." Christy nods and goes into the bathroom—my bathroom—and doesn't come out for a long time.

"This is temporary, Jeff," my mom says. As if I were begging to have Christy move in.

"I'm not the one who suggested she stay here tonight," I remind Mom.

"What would you have done if you'd answered the door? Told her she couldn't come in? Let her sleep in the garage? What?"

"No. But don't blame me for her staying here, that's all."

"Well, I doubt if she'd be here if it weren't for you! I've got a test in my intensive care nursing class tomorrow night and I can't concentrate at all right now."

We bicker back and forth until we hear the bathroom door open, then we stop and pretend to be watching TV. Christy comes out in my mom's nightgown and sits in a chair opposite me, brushing her long, wet hair. Her eyes are puffy from crying.

After my mom says goodnight, I go sit on the arm of Christy's chair. I take the brush from her and brush the back of her hair. "I'm sorry for the way things are," I say.

"Me, too," she sighs.

I brush her hair for a long time, smelling its cleanness, feeling the fine texture. She leans against me, then turns her face toward me. I kiss her red cheek, her toothpaste-tasting mouth. I don't mean to. It happens. That's all. She stands and pulls me toward her. I feel her nakedness under the nightgown, feel her full breasts. She holds me tight, leans into me, tightens her grip on my butt. We move to the sofa bed and lie on our sides, facing each other, as close as we can get. She guides my hand under her nightgown to the dampness between her legs.

"I love you, Jeff."

"I love you," I tell her.

She unbuttons my Levis, and we do, quietly and quickly, the deed that got us in so much trouble in the first place. After we lie together for a while, I tiptoe into my own room.

Do I really love her? I don't know. We've been together so long, she's like a habit. I always feel like I love her, when I say it. But now? Now I've got that tied-down, closed-in feeling again. If I really loved her, I don't think I'd be feeling so down right now. Would I?

7

By the end of the week practically everybody in the whole school knows Christy is pregnant. Kim and her other friend, Dana, are always patting her on the stomach and saying, "How cute." It makes me want to puke.

I'm trying to keep my distance from Christy, figure out some stuff, but it's hard, what with her staying with us.

Kelly, the girl who sits across from me in English, is acting cold. Last week, when I had my breaking-up speech all planned and thought I would soon be free, I'd fantasized about walking around Old Town with Kelly, checking out the Espresso Bar, just hanging out.

I hadn't asked her out or anything, or even mentioned that I was breaking up with Christy. But we talked a lot in English, and kind of flirted with each other. Right now she's flirting with Ray, who sits behind her. I don't care. It was a stupid fantasy anyway. I don't even like espresso coffee.

Mrs. Rosenbloom is handing out test papers and I notice that most of the kids already have theirs. This is not a good sign, since she always hands them back in order, from highest to lowest grades.

"Sixty-two percent," she says as she hands me my paper. "What happened to you, Jeff?"

I shrug.

The bell rings but Mrs. Rosenbloom says, "One moment, class." Still standing by my desk, frowning down at me, she warns us, "Sometimes seniors get lazy their last semester. I must caution you not to let up. Most of you in here are college bound—act like it!"

I get one low grade all year and she decides to lecture the whole class. I grab my books and push my way out the door, practically running into Coach Petersen.

"Hey Brownout. How's the Masterdebater?" he says, making it sound like masturbator.

That does it. I've taken enough shit for the week. Instead of going to fourth period, I find Benny.

"Let's split, Dude," I say.

"You mean now?" Benny says, looking at me like I'm crazy.

"Yeah, now. Right now."

"Sounds good to me," he says, a smile growing across his face.

When we get in the car and start driving, Benny says, "I can't believe it. Mr. Schoolboy's starting the weekend early." He laughs and punches me. "What made you decide to have some fun?"

"Coach Petersen's a dick," I say.

"So? What's new?"

"He's still ticked off because I dropped football and stayed in debate. It's not like I could do both and work twenty-five hours a week at the Fitness Club. I'm sure I'm going to choose football and lose a debate scholarship? I don't think so. I should just have told him, 'Get real, dick.' And old lady Rosenbloom decides to use my one low test score as a reason to lecture the whole class on the short-comings of seniors. And . . ."

"Hey. Chill out," Benny says. "Where are we going?"

I have been paying no attention to where I'm driving. We're practically to Foothill Boulevard.

"Let's go up to Angeles Flats," I say.

"Cool," Benny says. "You know, you can't let stuff get you down. You've got to take it a day at a time, like me."

"No offense, B.D., but you're not exactly my role model."

"Role model?" he says, looking puzzled. "I don't get it."

"My point exactly," I say.

"Hey, should we go back for Jeremy?"

"He wouldn't leave early."

"That's what I thought about you," Benny says with a laugh.

"Yeah, but Jeremy *really* wouldn't."

Neither of us says anything for about a mile, then I ask the question that's been on my mind.

"Have you heard about Christy?"

"Christy? Your Christy?"

"Yeah. *My* Christy," I say, sarcastically.

"No. What about her?"

"You sure you didn't hear about her?"

"No, Dude. What's to hear?"

"I thought everyone knew," I say.

"Knew what? You want me to play twenty questions? Is it animal, vegetable or mineral?"

"Animal, I guess . . . She's pregnant."

"Christy is?"

"Yeah."

"Hey. Cool. You're gonna be a dad."

Benny has this stupid grin on his face, like I've just told him I won the lottery or something.

"God, Benny. You can be such an idiot sometimes."

"You're not happy?"

"NO, I'M NOT HAPPY! Geez, why would I be happy?"

"I don't know. I might be happy if my girlfriend was pregnant."

"You don't have a girlfriend," I point out to him.

"Yeah. But I'm saying if . . ."

"You also don't have any plans for your life. I've got a lot I want to do before I have to turn into Mr. Responsibility."

"I'd be happy," he says, and I remember thinking a long time ago that Benny sort of liked Christy—just the way he joked around with her sometimes. None of us would ever try to cut in on somebody else's girl, but for a while I thought that if Christy and I ever broke up, Benny would be there waiting.

"We should go back for Jeremy," Ben says.

"What? We're halfway there."

"I don't care. This is a big deal. Turn the car around. C'mon."

Benny grabs the wheel and pulls it to the right.

"Benny! Watch what you're doing!"

"I'm serious. We've got to go back for Jeremy," he says. "Happy or not, this is a big event. The first of us to hit the target with our awesome sperm."

"God, you're a butthead," I say.

"Yeah, but I'm the one you wanted to leave school with. Huh!"

We go back to get Jeremy. I'm sure he won't come, but I park in front of the school and Benny jumps out. He's back with Jeremy before the narcs even notice.

"Pregnant?" Jeremy says.

I nod.

"For sure?" he says.

"For sure."

"My most sincere condolences," Jeremy says.

On the way to the mountains, Benny tells me to stop at a Seven-Eleven. He runs in and comes back with three six-packs.

"Celebration time," he says, pulling a beer from the carton.

"Don't open that in here," I tell him.

"Hey, what's the difference? We're illegal, open or not."

"Just don't."

"Okay," he says. "We're almost there, anyway."

We park in the Angeles Flats turnout, then walk down a gulley and up a hill on the other side. We sit on the top, on a big flat rock. The air is clear today so we can see beyond the high rises of downtown Los Angeles and the clump of skyscrapers at Century City, all the way to the ocean. Benny and I can even see the outline of Catalina Island. Jeremy can't make out the island because he has very poor distance vision. Benny hands us each a beer.

"You didn't steal these, did you?" Jeremy asks.

"No, why do you say that?"

"I can't imagine anyone selling it to you."

Benny pulls out his wallet and shows us his brother's I.D.

"Twenty-one. No problem," Benny smiles.

I hardly ever drink beer, or anything alcoholic. I've seen people do some amazingly stupid stuff when they're drunk. Besides, I don't much like the taste. But I'm thirsty, so I take the beer from Benny and tip it back for a long swig. The sun is warm overhead. A ridge to the east is charred and barren looking from the fires last October, but directly below us and to the west the trees are beginning to show fresh green growth.

This is the first place I brought Jeremy and Benny after I got my car. When we were little kids, in Scouts, we camped up here a couple of times. We've had some great times up here. At night it can be a party place, but right now we're the only ones here. You can see down in the gully though, beer cans and broken bottles, empty styrofoam food containers, dirty diapers—I hate that.

"Hey, why so down?" Benny says. "At least you know you're not shooting blanks."

"I wish I had been."

"Are you sure Christy won't consider an abortion?"

Jeremy says.

"Ah, that's cold, Dude. I'd never want a girlfriend of mine to have an abortion. It's his *baby*, J.J."

"I don't want a *baby*, Ben! Maybe when I'm thirty or something but not now!"

"You're cold. You're both cold," Ben says, downing his beer and opening another.

"It's stupid to have a baby now," Jeremy says to Benny. "Look at Christy. What's her life going to be like?"

"My sister had a baby when she was sixteen," Ben says.

"Oh yeah, your sister," Jeremy says. "That's different."

"What's that supposed to mean?"

"Well, you know. It's not exactly like your sister was working on getting a life. She was spending about an hour a week in Independent Studies and the rest of the time watching 'General Hospital' and 'Oprah'."

"So what? You learn a lot from that stuff. Not everybody has to be a brain like you. There's a lot more to life than school, Narrow Shoulders."

"Whatever you say, BB Brain."

I'm only half listening, looking down on the 210 Freeway, now more crowded with cars than when we first got here. They move in and out, passing, changing lanes, as if all governed by the same rhythm, the same beat. It's a dance. But if one car misses the beat, moves too soon to the next lane, there may be tragedy. That's how life is—one wrong move and the whole thing is screwed up. One wrong move.

"Earth to J.B., Earth to J.B. Come in J.B." Jeremy is holding a beer as if it's a walky-talky. I take it from him and open it, placing my empty can in the carton in front of Ben.

"My mom went to school with this girl who had an abortion and she died from it," Ben says.

"Your mom died from her friend's abortion?" Jeremy says in mock disbelief.

"You know what I mean, dick nose," Benny says, tossing

a handful of dirt at Jeremy. "It really happened," he says, turning to me.

"Your mom was in school in the old coat hanger days," I say. "People don't die from abortions anymore."

"Sometimes they do," Benny insists.

"Well, Christy won't because she's not having an abortion. It's stupid to talk about it," I say.

I slide off the rock and walk along the ridge a ways. Pine needles crunch under my feet, releasing a scent that makes the earth seem clean. I sit on the ground and finish my beer, then go back to where Jeremy and Benny are sitting. They're arguing about God. Benny believes in God. Jeremy is a total atheist. As usual, I'm somewhere in the middle.

"My sister had this wart on her little finger, and she prayed every day that the wart would go away, and it did."

"This is the same sister who watches 'Oprah,' right?"

"Yeah. But her wart went away!"

"Listen, B.D. What you're saying is there is this god who cures teeny, tiny warts while he lets twelve million children starve every year."

"Maybe he's just a wart god," I say. Then I laugh. And then I can't stop laughing. Benny and Jeremy start, too.

"He's buzzed," Benny says, and that makes me laugh harder. I'm laughing so hard tears are rolling down my cheeks. Jeremy has this snorting kind of laugh that makes things funnier still. We're sitting here on this rock, watching the lights come on in the valleys, and everything in the world is funny.

Gradually we gain control. Benny opens another beer for each of us. I notice we're on the second six-pack.

Jeremy wipes his eyes. "Oh, my goodness, gracious," he says, using another of his grandfatherly expressions. "Here's a joke."

The thought of one of Jeremy's weird jokes gets us laughing again.

"No. Don't laugh yet," Jeremy says.

We laugh harder.

"If you don't stop laughing, I won't tell it."

"Okay, okay," I say, still laughing.

Jeremy waits. When we are finally quiet he says, "This frog goes into a savings and loan place, hops up on the counter and asks for a loan from the teller. 'I'm only a teller. I can't give you a loan. You'll have to see our loan officer, Miss Wack.'"

"Miss Wack?" Benny starts laughing again. "Miss Wack-off?"

"No. Come on," Jeremy says. "Stop laughing . . . So anyway, the frog goes into Miss Wack's office, fills out the loan papers, and says 'Now can I get my loan?'

"The loan officer looks over the papers and says, 'These look fine, but you'll have to have some collateral.'

"'What do you mean, collateral?' the frog says.

"'You know. Something of value.'

"So the frog leaves and comes back about an hour later with this little statue of a fly on a lily pad and offers it as collateral. The loan officer takes one look at it and says no way will she give a loan on that basis.

"So the frog starts hopping all around, yelling in his hoarse voice, 'I want my loan! I want my loan!'

"Finally, the bank president comes in to see what all the commotion is about. The loan officer explains the whole thing and holds up the little statue. 'This is supposed to be his collateral. What is it anyway?'

"And the bank president takes the little statue and examines it carefully, then he tells her, 'it's a knick-knack, Patty Wack, give the frog a loan.'"

Jeremy doubles up with laughter. Ben and I look at each other.

"Don't you get it? It's a knick-knack Patty Wack, give the frog a loan!" Jeremy shouts. "C'mon you guys. Laugh! It's funny!" He sings the punch line to the tune of "This Old Man," and Benny and I sit and look at him. Finally though, we can stand it no longer and we both burst out laughing at the same time. And then we all sing it together.

It's dark now, and the stars are out. It's a full moon, and Jeremy is going on about gravity and the moon and tides. When we get tired of Jeremy's scholarly lecture, Ben and I sing at the top of our lungs, "It's a knick-knack, Patty Wack..." which prompts uncontrollable laughter from the three of us. Then Jeremy gets the hiccups, which *really* makes us laugh.

There are two more cars parked in the turn-out, but we haven't seen any other people. We're on our last can of beer. I slide down from the rock.

"Gotta take a leak," I say, walking down to the closest tree.

Benny lets out a big burp, then yells, "Hey, keep that thing in your pants unless you've got a rubber handy."

I hear them both laughing, then drown out the noise by letting go with a steady stream against the tree trunk. I'm down to the last drop when suddenly I'm blinded by a flashlight shining in my face. I turn my head.

"Hey!" I say.

"Hey, yourself," a gruff voice says. The flashlight is aimed away from me, and I get a good look at a ranger. He's so big, if it weren't for his uniform I'd have thought Bigfoot found me.

"Oh, shit," I say.

"You want to do that, too? Go ahead. I've got time."

I zip up.

"You boys been having a little party up here?"

"No, just talking," I say.

"Right." He shines the flashlight back in my face, looking into my eyes. Then he has me do that thing where you put your head back and touch your fingers to your nose. I keep missing my nose.

"What's your name?"

I tell him. He asks for an I.D. and I hand over my wallet.

"Okay, Jeff, come along with me," he says, flashing an official-looking badge. My heart is pounding so hard I think he can see it, but I try to stay cool.

"Where are you taking me?"

"You and your friends get to go back to the ranger station," he says.

I notice that's he's carrying a club, and although he hasn't been nasty, he's scary looking. We walk back to the turnout. Benny and Jeremy and another ranger are crowded into the back seat of an old, beat-up Jeep.

"You boys been drinking some, I see," the ranger who's driving says.

"Not much," Benny says.

"Three six-packs of twelve-ouncers? I'd say that's enough to get drunk and disorderly on."

"Disorderly?" Benny says.

"Yep. We got a call about noise up here."

Jeremy says, "So, is it against the law to laugh up here? I saw the 'No smoking' sign. Did I miss the no laughing sign?"

"Don't get smart with me," the ranger says, "or you'll find yourself booked officially down at the sheriff's station."

I turn back to look at Jeremy and Benny. Please keep your mouths shut, I think.

We bounce along over a dirt road until we come to this little house kind of place. There are two chairs, two desks, and some ranger paraphernalia—binoculars, maps, a compass.

"Where's Smoky Bear?" Ben says, then he does this fake kid cry, "Smoky, Smoky, I wanna see Smoky, Ranger Rick."

I really wish Ben would shut up.

The Bigfoot ranger walks over to Ben and stands real close, looking down at him.

"Listen, Buddy, you got caught by the good guys. We want everybody to be safe and happy up here, and not to misuse their national resources. But you've broken the law, and if I hear any more of this Ranger Rick, Smoky

Bear crap we'll drive down the hill and let the sheriff hold you three knick-knackers in a cell for a while."

I'm relieved that Ben doesn't come up with any more smart-ass remarks. The three of us sit on a wooden bench and listen while the other ranger, the smaller one, makes phone calls.

Benny's mom is home and so is Jeremy's dad, so they get picked up in about thirty minutes. But my mom isn't home, and I end up waiting and waiting. It's cold in the ranger station. I have a nasty taste in my mouth. Nothing seems so funny anymore. Finally, the ranger reaches my mom. It is after midnight when she comes to get me. Steve is with her. She doesn't look happy to see me.

"**Y**ou better try to get a grip on yourself, Jeffrey Dean Browning, or things are going to get worse and worse!"

Mom clenches the steering wheel tightly as she maneuvers the curves of Angeles Crest Highway.

"I can't take much more of this," she says. "It seems like it's been one crisis after another with you lately. I'm worried sick about you—drinking in the mountains? I suppose you were then going to get in your car and attempt to drive home?"

My head is spinning.

"It's lucky Steve was still at the house when the rangers called so he could come up with me and drive your car back. You sure as hell couldn't."

My palms are clammy. Sweat is dripping from my forehead.

"Pull over, Mom."

"Why?" she asks, then glances at me.

She pulls abruptly to the side of the road. I barely have time to open the door when I barf up beer, lunch, breakfast, my toes, it feels like.

Steve, in my car, screeches to a halt behind us and comes sprinting up.

"Everything okay?" he asks.

I've still got my head hanging out the car door.

"Karen?"

I hear him open the door on Mom's side. I wipe my mouth on my sleeve and sit up. Steve has his arms around my mom and her back is shaking with silent sobs.

"It's okay, Sis," he says. "Remember your prom?"

Mom stiffens and pulls away from him.

"The mess this boy's in is hardly an innocent dance with one bottle of champagne poured into eight gallons of Hawaiian Punch," she says.

"I'll take him home with me tonight," he says.

"Gladly," she says, sounding tired.

Steve looks over at me. "Come on, Jeff. Let's give your mom a break."

I get out, walk back to my car and climb in on the passenger side.

I pull the pillow over my face, blocking light. I'm not ready for morning. There is a foul taste in my mouth and a dull ache in my head. My feet hang over the end of the couch, exposed and cold. I turn over, first one side then the other. No way can I get comfortable, but I'm not ready to get up and face the day, either.

The phone rings and Steve answers.

"Still sleeping," he says softly.

"No . . . okay . . . sure . . . Shall I have him call you?"

I can tell it's my mom on the other end. I pull the pillow back over my head, blocking the sound, trying to block out my thoughts, my feelings, my messed-up life.

"What time do you have to be at work today?" Steve nudges my shoulder.

"Two. I've got the afternoon shift."

"Well, get up and move around. You'll feel better."

"What time is it?"

"Almost noon."

"Okay," I say, not moving.

"There's an unopened toothbrush in the medicine cabinet. I imagine you need one."

Steve's voice has an edge to it that I've not heard before. I drag myself off the couch and into the bathroom—brush my teeth, brush my tongue and take a long, hot shower. The scalding water feels good against my chest. I tip my head back under the shower, get a mouthful of hot water, and rinse. Yuck! The taste of stale beer and vomit doesn't go away.

"Here are some clean loaner clothes," Steve says, opening the door and dropping old sweats, a tee shirt and underwear on the counter. "I've dumped your clothes from last night in with a load I've got going."

"Thanks."

If my clothes smell anything like how my mouth tastes, I hope he used plenty of soap.

On the kitchen table there is a box of granola, milk, bananas, and a couple of bowls. Steve's apartment is kind of like a second home to me but today I don't feel so comfortable here. I sit at the table, across from him, and stare at the milk-soaked kernels of granola that lay uneaten in my bowl. Finally, Steve drops the sports section on the chair next to him and says, "Talk to me, Jeff."

I look up and sigh, "I don't know what to say."

"How about saying what's on your mind?"

"Nothing's on my mind."

"Yeah, right. Your girlfriend's pregnant, you got detained by rangers last night as a result of being shitfaced, and nothing's on your mind?"

What *can* I say? I sit, silent, feeling Steve's gaze resting heavy on me.

"Listen, Jeff. I'm on your side. Remember me? Uncle Steve? You're like a son to me. I want to help."

"I know. It's just . . . there's nothing I can do, that's all."

"What do you mean?"

"Well... I don't want Christy to have the baby. She won't even think about an abortion. So that's it. I mean, I'm not the kind of guy who's gonna go kick her in the stomach."

"And you're sure this is your baby?" Steve asks.

I nod my head yes. Christy flirts around sometimes, but I'd be lying if I said she'd ever been with anyone else. I know she hasn't.

"I hear Christy's dad wants the two of you to get married."

"Christy's dad is a nutcase. I don't want to get married."

"What about Christy? Does she want to get married?"

"I don't know. When she first told me she was pregnant she was all happy, like we were going to live happily ever after or something. Then when I told her I didn't want a baby she got totally wigged out—called me a baby killer—that stuff. She wouldn't even talk to me."

"But you must be talking now, if she's staying at your house."

"Yeah. Something happened. We sort of made up."

"You don't seem real happy about it."

So I tell Steve how I've been wanting to break up with Christy, and just as I had my nerve up to tell her so, she dropped the baby bomb on me. And I also tell him the reason I'd stopped using condoms was because Christy was on the pill.

"Oldest trick in the book," Steve says.

"What do you mean?"

"A guy starts to lose interest, the gal gets herself pregnant, then she's got him. They're connected forever."

"You mean you think Christy did it on purpose?"

"It's possible."

"But that's not fair!"

Steve laughs. "But it works."

"But Christy wants to go to college, be a teacher for deaf kids, stuff you can't do with a baby."

"Maybe she wants that. Maybe she wants you more."

I go to the sink, get a glass of water and down it. I've been super thirsty all morning.

"I don't think so, Steve. I don't think Christy would do that."

"Maybe she didn't exactly do it on purpose. Maybe she started worrying about losing you and just thought she'd leave things to fate—if it was meant to be, then it would happen."

My heart sinks. Christy is big on that what's meant to be will be stuff. When Steve puts it this way, I can see where she might just let things happen. God. Why? And why wasn't I more careful?

"When I was in high school," Steve says, "if a guy got his girlfriend pregnant he automatically married her as soon as possible, unless she moved in with a relative in some other state and put the baby up for adoption."

"Adoption?"

"Yeah. The girl would show up six or seven months later, back in school, as if nothing had happened."

I'd never thought about adoption! Maybe that's the answer! Steve must be thinking along the same lines.

"That might be a good thing for Christy," he says. "She's not going to have a way to take care of this baby, is she? It doesn't sound like her parents will help her out and I know your mom doesn't plan on adding major baby-sitting tasks to her life just as she's getting ready to start a new job at the hospital."

"Christy's mom might want to help, but her dad's the big boss in that family and he's wacko. He kicked her out of the house—she had to sneak back when he was at work so she could get some clothes. She doesn't really have anywhere to stay but with us."

"I know. Your mom says things are kind of crowded at your house now. It must be a bit awkward for you."

I nod, thinking of Wednesday night, and how Christy and I ended up in bed together. Although it felt good at the time, it had complicated things.

Steve and I talk on and on. He lectures me about drinking and driving.

"I know all that," I tell him.

"You knew to wear a condom, too," he says.

We talk about the debate tournament coming up, and the Lakers, and Steve's job, then after lunch we jump in the pool. I love California—riots, fires, earthquakes, smog, carjackings and all, because in the middle of February you can go for a swim and even, sometimes, have an outside barbeque in the evening.

When I was eleven my mom almost married a guy from Vermont. This is a whole other story, but anyway we stayed with him for the month of February. Everything was a big hassle. I had to spend hours getting dressed just to go to the corner market—gloves, boots, hat, the works. None of this jeans, tee shirt and sneaker stuff there. And half the time you couldn't even go *anywhere* because of snow or ice or a storm. I hated it. (The guy we were staying with wasn't so great, either. Luckily, Mom figured that out.)

After work, Mom is waiting for me in the parking lot.

"Come on. I want to talk to you," she says.

She still looks kind of mad. We go to a restaurant where we usually have a good time. It's this Chinese place where we get tons of food for not much money. As soon as we sit down she starts. I can tell this is not going to be fun.

"I am very upset with you, Jeffrey, to think you would get so drunk—that in the first place—but then that you would *drive?*"

"Mom, I didn't drive," I say, pointing out the obvious.

"Yes, but you would have. It's the same thing."

"What makes you think I would have driven?"

"According to the rangers, your friends were in no better shape than you were. Besides, Jeremy doesn't have a license yet and Benny sober is a menace to public safety when he gets behind the wheel of a car. How were you planning to get home, if not to drive?"

"I don't know, but at least I *didn't* drive."

"And I don't like you hanging around with Benny Dominguez anymore, either."

"What's wrong with Benny? You always act like you like him. Whenever he comes to the house you give him a hug, tell him to come back more often. Now all of a sudden you don't like him?"

"It's not that I don't like him. How can anyone not like Benny? He makes me laugh. He's always been a sweetheart as far as I'm concerned."

"So what's your problem with Benny?"

"Come on, Jeff. I don't live under a rock. I see him with that bunch of hoodlums that hang out down by the liquor store, over there on Seventh Street, whenever I drive past there on the way to or from the hospital. School hours, midnight, it doesn't matter, he's there looking tough."

"So, what's that got to do with me? You don't see me down on Seventh Street, do you?"

"No. But I've done my Emergency Room internship and I've seen kids who look just like Benny, same dress, same posture, being brought into Emergency, bleeding to death from gunshot wounds. And maybe they were the target, or maybe they were next to the target, or maybe they were playing pool in the target's garage, for gods sakes. At least have sense enough to stay away from Benny and his *homeboys*."

I didn't know anyone could get as much sarcasm into any one word as my mom just put into "homeboys."

When she finishes talking about what a fool I was last night, and what a fool I am to hang around with Benny, she starts on the whole pregnancy thing—how disappointed she is, how I'm ruining my future and Christy's future, too.

I eat my kung pao chicken and listen. Not only am I messing up for me and Christy, she talks like I'm messing up for her, too—she says how she can't get her paper done because Christy's there watching TV all the time, and how she can't concentrate on what she needs to learn for midterm exams. She says, "I've worked hard to get this far in school. I take my opportunities seriously, even if you don't."

"But I do, Mom. I'm working really hard in debate, so I can qualify for the Brooker University scholarship."

She sighs. "I don't know how you think you'll go off to school with all the responsibilities that go with being a father."

We both poke at our food, not eating, not talking. Then Mom says, "You know how much I love you, Jeff, and how much I want you to finish your education. But your little baby is going to need a lot of care. And I'm not willing to take that on. I've already told you that, and I mean it. Just as I finally get to a spot where I can do the kind of work I've always wanted—I'm not going to sacrifice a nursing career to be a full-time grandmother. I'm sorry."

"Mom! No one is asking you to sacrifice anything," I say.

"No, but I don't see any plan for this new baby. Christy says how much she already loves her little unborn baby, but I don't hear her saying anything about taking care of it, or supporting it, or working things out so she can finish school after it's born. It's like she's pregnant with a doll."

"I'm hoping she'll consider adoption," I say.

"I wish she would," Mom says. "But I don't believe that will happen. Christy and I have had a lot of talks since she's been staying at our place. I think she wants this baby very much. But I'm telling you, Jeff, I see these grandmothers, starting all over again with their baby's babies. I want you to understand, I can't do it. I just can't!"

And then she starts crying. Maybe I'm a coward, or embarrassed, I don't know, but I have to leave. Besides, the way my luck's been going, I'm afraid to see what the fortune cookie might say. I walk back to the Fitness Club where my car is still parked, then drive home and grab some clothes and my books.

"What are you doing?" Christy says as I walk past her back toward the door.

"Going back to Steve's."

"Come talk," she says in this kind of pleading voice.

"I've had enough talk for one day," I say.

"I don't get you," she yells after me. "You're all lovey-dovey one minute and then next you're the iceman!"

"I don't get *you*, either," I yell back without stopping. "You're on the pill one month and pregnant the next!"

Steve isn't home, so I use the key from under the mat. I get blankets and a pillow and flop down on the sofa. What a day. What a week. What now?

It feels strange to be staying at my uncle's house. I've stayed with him often, but never for more than one or two days at a time. But now, I've got my clothes hanging in his den closet, and he's moved a camp cot inside so I won't have to sleep with my feet hanging over the end of the couch. I've been here for three weeks. My mom wants me to come home, but I'm not going to do it until Christy finds somewhere else to stay.

See, if I go back to my house, and my mom is out, or already in bed, and Christy puts her arms around me, fresh from the shower and nothing on under her big, old tee shirt, I know what will happen. And then it will be like we're together, and we're having a baby together. And everything is so cute. I don't want that. So I'm at Steve's. When I first came here it was because my mom and I weren't getting along. But when he told me I could stay for a while, it seemed like a good idea, more because of Christy than because of my mom.

Sometimes, when I get out of school, or work, I find myself on Columbus Street, like I've been on automatic pilot and I've forgotten I don't live there right now. Then I turn around and go back to Steve's apartment.

I've told Christy I want some time to think things through, and I can't be with her right now. She said she hated me, but then two days later there was a note on my windshield saying she needed me to take her to her next doctor's appointment.

Saturday morning someone is banging on the door before I'm out of bed. I hear Steve stirring around so I stay in bed, listening. It's Mom.

"Hey, Karen. What brings you out so early?"

"Life," she says.

I hear them walking toward the kitchen, then hear the sounds of coffee being prepared. I'm in the camp bed, in the den, with the door closed, but Steve's apartment wasn't built for privacy and I can hear everything he and Mom are saying.

"What are you up to today, Steve?"

"Errands, grocery shopping, Saturday things. I may go to a movie this afternoon. Wanna join me?"

"No, thanks. But could I take refuge in your bedroom or kitchen or somewhere quiet? I can't seem to study at home anymore."

"Why not?"

"Oh, I don't know, Steve. Christy's there most of the time, watching TV. I swear if I hear one more piece of corny soap opera dialogue, I'm going to throw my iron skillet through the TV screen."

"Doesn't she do anything besides watch TV?"

"She eats. I feel sorry for her—sixteen, she's pregnant, her dad's kicked her out, and her boyfriend doesn't want anything more to do with her. Basically, she's a nice kid, but she's . . . well . . . underfoot."

"How much longer do you think she'll be with you?"

"I hope not much longer, but what can I do? She has no-where else to go. It's funny. Ever since I first met her, she's told me how nice it is to be in a house where people get along and aren't always yelling at each other, and now, there she is, moved in."

"Do you think she wants to stay there indefinitely?" Steve asks.

"Maybe. She doesn't seem to be in any hurry to leave. And now her mother, Olga, is over at my place half the time, too, crying, saying she misses her, she wants her home. I'm afraid they're both going to end up living with me. And I miss Jeff, but he won't come home while she's there. Can I come stay with you?"

They both laugh. They've got this strange brother/sister thing where they laugh alike, and they laugh at all the same stuff.

I lie there on the cot, thinking back to the last Labor Day barbeque we had in our backyard. My mom always does a back-to-school barbeque. Christy, Stacy, Jeremy and Benny were all there. Uncle Steve fixed the hamburgers and a bunch of my mom's friends from work came and brought food. After dinner we all played kick-the-can, like a bunch of little kids. Then, at nine o'clock, Christy's dad called and demanded she come straight home.

"Why does he have to be like that?" she'd said. "He's mad because he wanted me home at eight-thirty. He says I'm grounded for two weeks." Then she'd started to cry. "I'd give anything to have a family like yours and to live where people care about each other and they don't fight all the time. Anything," she'd said.

I turn my attention back to the conversation that is drifting through the wall.

"Christy may be basically a nice kid. I think she is. But she sure tricked Jeff, don't you think?" Steve asked.

"Probably. But how could he be so goddamned stupid?" Mom said, sounding very angry.

"Karen, you've got to forgive him. He made a mistake."

"I know. I know. I'm trying. But he's got so much ahead of him—the scholarship, and he's so good at so many things. He's always had such a good heart. The only trouble he's ever given me was about mowing the lawn. Really, Steve, the whole world was opening before him, and now what? His prospects have shrunk like wool in a hot dryer."

I can't lie here listening anymore. I get up and walk into the kitchen, rubbing my eyes as if I've just awakened. Mom stands up and hugs me. I hug her back, hard.

"I miss you, Jeffie. Come home," she says.

"I can't, Mom. Not yet."

Thursday afternoon I take Christy to the doctor. She wants me to come in with her, listen to the baby's heart through this special kind of stethoscope thing, but I don't want to. I'm only taking her because there's no one else to do it and I feel guilty. I wait in the car, in the parking lot, and watch people come and go. Some of the women who go in there are huge, and they waddle, like ducks. I wonder if Christy will get like that.

After about two hours Christy comes walking out, all smiles.

"Everything's fine," she says. "I have to start taking these iron pills, but that's maybe because I haven't been eating right."

I sit there looking at her. She seems happy. How can she be happy?

"Hey, Christy. I've been talking with my Uncle Steve about adoption. He says there are lots of people who can't have kids and who can offer great homes to babies. What do you think?"

Christy's smile fades. "I think you're an idiot! I always looked up to you so, but you're a person with no heart. How could you want to give our baby to strangers, and never ever see it again? What kind of person are you, anyway?"

"I just thought it would be a good idea. We can't take care of it, give it to someone who can."

"This is a little person, Jeff, not a baby kitten."

"I can get some information. Would you at least think

about it?"

"I don't want your information!"

"But what are you going to do? How will you support it? What kind of life will it have? What about college?"

"I don't *care* about college right now. Okay?"

"Okay, Christy. Okay. But I'm not in this with you. I'm not going to play house with you. I'm going to live my life."

"Get me pregnant and run out! That's the kind of person you are!"

"You got you pregnant!"

"Ha! How could I do that?"

"By pretending to be on the pill!"

"You don't know anything!"

"I know I don't want a baby! I know I want a free life! I know I don't want to be with you anymore!"

Well . . . it's not the way I'd planned to say it, but it's out. Christy turns her head away from me. I drive her back to my house. Neither of us speaks until I turn into the driveway.

"Wait just a minute," she says. "I'm going to get my things and go home."

"But Christy . . ."

She opens the door with the extra key my mom gave her. She goes to my room where I guess she's been staying. Clothes, shampoo, books, all are stuffed into three grocery bags which we then carry to the car.

"What about your dad?" I say.

"My mother told me a few days ago that he wants me to come home."

"Really? Does my mom know?"

"No . . . " She looks as if she might say more. I wait for more explanation, but none comes. I drive her home and help carry in the shopping bags. Her mother runs from the kitchen, throws her arms around Christy and welcomes her home. I think she welcomes her home—she is speaking Spanish, but it seems like a welcome. Her dad sits in his chair, in front of the TV, watching Christy and her mom.

Neither of them speak to me.

Maria comes in from the kitchen and says to Christy, "Don't think you're getting your old room back!"

I leave. A sense of freedom comes over me as I drive away—lonely freedom.

10

The day after Christy and I officially break up is the day I'm scheduled to do my dramatic interpretation piece in the debate class. This is one of the two events that will get me to nationals. And nationals will get me the Brooker University scholarship. I don't have to win anything in the national tournament, I just have to qualify and compete.

"Ready, Jeff?" Mr. Rogers says, just after I walk in.

"Now?"

"Might as well."

I wait until the bell rings, then stand at the front of the classroom, waiting for silence. I don't let my eyes wander to the place in the room where I know Christy is sitting. I begin:

> *"I told my father not to worry, that love is what matters, and that in the end, when he is loosed from his body, he can look back and say without blinking that he did all right by me, his son, and that I loved him . . ."*
>
> *From the short story, "The Year of Getting to Know Us," by Ethan Canin . . .*

I can feel it. The introduction, the cut, the blend of

humor and sadness—it all works and, for the purpose of
this D.I., I become the character, Leonard, from the short
story, whose dad hardly knows him, hardly cares. When I
finish, I stand very still making the transition from Leonard
back to myself.

"Great, Jeff," Mr. Rogers says. "It's an unusual choice,
but I think that's to your advantage for this tournament—
Comments?"

I stand, waiting. This is the time people say, "I really
liked how you used your hands . . ." or . . . "Great voice
distinction between characters . . ." or . . . "Wow!"

I know I got it right. I'm jazzed! I can see it in Roger's
face, too. But when I look at the other faces, no one is even
looking at me, except Jeremy.

"Hey, what goes here?" Mr. Rogers says. "How about
giving this guy a little feedback?"

"Cassie? . . . Dashan? . . . Patrick?" Mr. Rogers calls on
the kids who always have something to say, but this time
they don't.

No one looks up. Kim leans forward, whispers something to Christy, and pats her on the shoulder. Christy
smiles a weak-looking smile and suddenly, I get it. I am the
bad guy. No one's saying anything because they don't want
to be nice to me.

Mr. Rogers is standing there, looking puzzled, but I'm
not puzzled. Inside my head I'm screaming "It's not my
fault!" But outside, I'm cool, still waiting for someone to
say something. No one does. Okay. Okay. I don't need
them. I grab my books and hurry out of the room.

The weekend after Christy moves back to her house, I
move back to mine. It's good to be home, sleeping in my own
soft bed, listening to my own private stereo. Nothing
against my Uncle Steve's taste in music—he's got a right
to like what he likes, but I don't think I could take one more
playing of that country-western dude singing about how

he's got friends in low places, especially not with Steve singing along.

When Steve first played that song for me, I thought it was kind of clever. But that was a long time ago, and he still plays it all the time. Last week I told him, give it a rest, but he reminded me that it was *his* stereo, and *his* apartment. Anyway, it's good to be home, and listening to a little Pearl Jam, and some old-time classic rock.

I guess the music I first noticed was stuff like The Beatles, The Who, The Rolling Stones. That's what my mom used to play when I was a little, little kid. She'd dance me around, both of us laughing, to "It's a Hard Day's Night," and "Eleanor Rigby."

My grandma thinks Elvis is king, but maybe she didn't dance me around to him enough, or something, because I don't really enjoy listening to him. Now my mom listens to New Wave, which pretty much puts me to sleep. But I still like the old stuff I cut my teeth on.

Jeremy has started listening to jazz in preparation for being in New Orleans for the national debate tournament. How's that for confidence? He hasn't even qualified for nationals yet and he's preparing for the trip. He keeps stopping by my house and leaving tapes of John Coltrane and Duke Ellington, whoever they are. I'm not into them yet. Maybe I will be if it turns out that for sure I'm going to New Orleans in June.

The first night I'm back home, Sunday night, Mom brings in pizza and Stacy comes over. We don't talk much. After dinner Mom says, "I'm meeting with my study group tonight. See you later." She pats me on the shoulder on her way out. "I'm happy you're home again, Jeff," she says. But her voice sounds flat, not happy.

As soon as mom leaves, Stacy says, "I hear you broke up with Christy."

"Yeah, I did."

"Kim was going on and on about it in gym on Friday—how everybody thought you were such a good guy and you turned out to be a jerk."

"I don't give a shit what Kim says," I say.

"Kim's acting like the great protector right now. 'Christy, be careful, don't strain yourself . . . Did you eat a good breakfast this morning, little mommie?' It's disgusting."

"Yeah, well . . . Kim's always been sort of weird."

"You'd think *she* was the dad," Stacy says.

"I wish!"

We talk for a while, getting caught up with each other. I've hardly seen Stacy for the past three weeks, while I've been at Steve's. She tells me how Frankie got fired again. Frankie's had about eighteen jobs since she first started going around with him.

"What was it for this time?"

"He was handing out free donuts to his friends."

"Isn't that how he got fired from Wendy's, only for handing out hamburgers?" I ask.

"Yeah."

"Your boyfriend's a slow learner," I say.

"I'm not pregnant," she says, laughing. "But, speaking of Frankie, he's coming over tonight. See ya."

"Bye," I say, following her out the door.

I get in the car and head for Jeremy's house. One thing about having a really brainy friend—he's always at home. I walk around to the back of his house and tap on his bedroom window. He opens it.

"Hey, J.B. Come on in."

He opens the window and I climb through. It's easier than walking through the house. Jeremy's mom always wants to talk to me for about an hour, and his dad always looks at me like he can't quite remember who I am. They're strange. I mean, they're Jeremy's parents and I guess he likes them okay. He never says anything one way or the other about them. They're nice enough. But I can skip seeing them.

"What's that smell?" I ask.

"Smell? I don't smell anything," Jeremy says.

"God, it's rank in here."

"It's just my room," Jeremy says, puzzled.

"Yeah," I say. "It's been a while since I've been here. Maybe I've just forgotten how a budding zoologist's room smells."

"If I were budding, it would be a botanist's room," Jeremy laughs.

I look around. There are three separate hamster cages, and two cages for rats. They all look alike to me, but Jeremy knows each one by name.

"I had to isolate Olivia," Jeremy says, pointing to the smallest rat, curled in the corner of a cage. "Byron was eating her tail."

"That's gross!"

"Nature, my man. Simply nature. I'll probably feed her to Beatrice in a few days, anyway. The fact that her tail is shorter than it was is not important."

Beatrice is the boa that Jeremy's had for about five years now. Most of the time it lives curled up in a big glass cage, but sometimes he wears it around his neck while he's sitting at his desk. His mom freaks out when she sees that.

Besides the snake and the hamsters, Jeremy has a tortoise, a chameleon and an aquarium full of bright-colored tropical fish. Oh, yeah, and a white rabbit with pink eyes. The rabbit uses a kitty litter box. That's one thing in here that doesn't smell so good.

"I liked your D.I. the other day," Jeremy says.

"Yeah, well, thanks a lot," I say, sarcastically. "Why didn't you say that in class?"

"I don't like to talk in class unless it's official. You know that."

"But you're my friend. You should have stood up for me."

"I'm your friend," Jeremy says. "But I'm not like this guy." He picks the chameleon up from the drab rock it's been sitting on and puts it down in a nest of bright green leaves. We watch it slowly change color.

"I am who I am, and I don't talk in class unless called upon."

"Have you finished writing your speech for San Diego?" I ask.

"I've just got to gather a few statistics to prove my point."

"What is your point?"

"The crime rate would drop dramatically if all drugs were legalized."

"Yeah," I say, laughing. "Everyone would be so spaced out, no one could figure out how to do a crime."

Jeremy gives his rationale. Crime rates are much lower in Denmark, where there is a very lenient approach to drug use. People don't have to steal to get drugs because so much is available through government programs. Instead of all the money going into "the war on drugs," money could be going into rehabilitation, and so forth. Then he says, "I'm sorry, my man, I should have said something the other day in debate—backed you up."

"Oh, it's okay," I say. "Everyone's talking to me again, anyway, except Kim and Christy. In fact, Dashan and Cassie both called that evening to tell me they thought it went well."

"Yeah, well, after you walked out, Rogers really chewed us out."

"He did?"

"Seriously. He said if anyone in that class had a personal problem with you, or anyone else for that matter, they'd better work it out because our group has to pull together no matter what—we've got to support each other or we're lost."

"The usual winning's not as important as being decent people stuff?"

"Yeah, but what started it was how no one gave you any response to your presentation. He also gave us a mini-lecture about not judging someone until you've walked a mile in their moccasins."

About eleven o'clock we go over to Benny's. He and his brother, Gilbert, are in the garage, working on Benny's car, which hasn't run for the past six months.

Gilbert looks up. "It's your two smart friends," he says to Benny, who still has his head under the hood, examining some pump or something. He stands and looks at us, smiling.

"One smart friend and one not as smart as we used to think," he says, laughing and wiping grease from his hands.

"Time to call it a night," Gilbert says, waving and walking toward the house.

"Hey, thanks, Gil. Maybe tomorrow night we can start her up?"

"Maybe."

I reach down and pick up a triangular shaped, shiny chrome part to something.

"What's this?" I say, holding it out toward Benny.

He takes it from me, turns it over in his hand several times, grins, and says, "It's a knick-knack, Patty Wack, give the frog a loan."

Jeremy and I both groan in unison, then we all start laughing.

"God, I'm still in trouble for that with my old man," Ben says. "Practically every day he leaves some AA pamphlet sitting around where I have to see it. Like on my dresser, or taped to the refrigerator."

"My mother spoke with fervor about how I shouldn't hang around people of low caliber," Jeremy says.

"I thought she liked me," I say.

"She was probably talking about Benny," Jeremy laughs.

"I got lectured from my mom *and* Steve," I say. "But I guess they're not mad anymore."

"We ought to go up there again. Maybe tomorrow," Benny says. "I can always buy beer, and we just need to go up a little farther past the ranger station."

Jeremy and I both stare at him. I know I don't want a

repeat experience of that Friday night. I don't think Jeremy does either.

"Just an idea," Benny says. "Don't take life so serious. Lighten up . . . Hey, how about shooting some pool?"

We move the car parts out of the way so we won't stumble on stuff, and set up the pool table. We're pretty evenly matched. After a while we put up the cue sticks and get some sodas from the old refrigerator at the back of the garage.

"Things are going to be really different without you guys around here next year," Benny says. "All I'll have left are my low-life friends."

"What do you think you'll end up doing next year?" Jeremy asks.

"I don't know. Maybe graduating from high school."

We all laugh at that.

"Really?" Jeremy says.

"Nah. I'm failing history right now, but I can pull it out at the last minute—that's probably what you thought, too, huh Jeff? Pull out at the last minute?"

Ben laughs so hard he starts to choke.

"No, you bozo comedian, I didn't pull out. Damn it! Christy said she was on the pill!"

"You know the only sure way the pill works?" Benny says, still sputtering. "It's if the girl always holds the pill between her knees."

"Geez, Benny," I say, throwing a grease rag at him. He just keeps laughing. Jeremy stands back watching us, as if he's an anthropologist observing weird tribal behavior. We go back to pool.

After a while Benny says, "I may join the Army after graduation."

"How primitive," Jeremy says.

"No. Let's face it, I've screwed up all through school. You guys both are set for college and jobs. The only skill I've developed is how to get by."

"But the Army?" Jeremy says. "Why not go to Hamilton

Heights City College? They'd take you."

"Nah. I hate school. Really, I'd rather go to Basic Training than sit in some boring class. Besides, I want to be all that I can be," he says, quoting the standard recruiting line.

We play more pool, talk, laugh and horse around until Benny's dad comes out.

"It's after one, you guys. Time to break it up." He eyes us suspiciously, picks up Benny's can of soda and sniffs it, as if expecting to find something other than Pepsi, then he turns and goes back into the house. Benny laughs.

"My old man thinks just because *he* was a big time alcoholic, I'm gonna be the same."

On the way home Jeremy asks me, "How does it feel not to be with Christy anymore?"

"It's great. Like tonight. If I'd still been with Christy there would have been a big hassle about why wasn't I at her place on a Sunday night, or she'd be calling my house, wanting to know why I was out so late. I don't want to have to answer to anyone again, ever."

"I know what you mean," Jeremy says. "My brief foray into the world of relationships with Trish last year left me knowing I was not yet ready for the trappings of love."

"Trappings is right," I say.

So here I am, back in my own bed, the stereo turned down low, ready for sleep. It felt good, being with Ben and Jeremy tonight, laughing and messing around. Free. I feel free. But there's this other feeling, too—a feeling of emptiness inside—a feeling I don't want to think about. I wonder if there will ever be a time in my life when I'm not confused?

11

March 14. It's finally here. The debate tournament in which I will qualify for nationals, or not—receive a scholarship, or not. Usually I don't get nervous, but this tournament is a different story.

Last night, when I finally got to sleep after about four hours of tossing and turning, I had this very weird dream. Hundreds of people were watching me give my D.I. I was getting to the really sad, intense part, the part where everybody usually gets very quiet, and I heard people in the audience giggling. I tried to put more emotion into it, make them see how sad it was, but they laughed all the more. Then I looked down. I wasn't wearing any pants. I was naked from the waist down. I tried to cover myself, but the whole audience was laughing uproariously. I tried to run from the room, but I couldn't get the door open. I awoke, shaking and drenched with sweat, glad it was nearly time to get up.

Mr. Rogers blasts the horn on the rented van, and I grab my backpack and duffle bag and run out. We've each had to contribute thirty-two dollars to pay for the van. Every now and then Mr. Rogers climbs on his soapbox and carries on about how the football team, which hasn't won a game since WWII, gets thousands of dollars worth of bus transportation at the expense of the school district, and the debate team, which is one of the top-rated teams in the state, has to take up collections to get to tournaments.

Jeremy is already in the back seat, along with Hung, and Dashan. I take the middle seat, behind Mr. Rogers. We stop for Trin, then go on to Christy's.

At first the principal, Mr. Hill, told Rogers that Christy couldn't go on any official school trips because she was pregnant. Something about school liability. To tell the truth, I was secretly relieved when I first heard that piece of news, but then I changed my mind.

Rogers went nuts when Mr. Hill tried to keep Christy off the debate trip. He said the school was discriminating against pregnant students. Then everyone in the class worked on a petition, which cited Supreme Court cases upholding the rights of pregnant students, and we got over six hundred student, teacher, and parent signatures on it. So Mr. Hill decided to let Christy go. Rogers said it was an example of democracy in action.

I worked on getting the petition signed, too. Even though I feel really awkward around Christy now, and she doesn't speak to me, and neither do her girlfriends, I know it's not right to keep her from participating in debate tournaments just because she's pregnant.

Christy grabs the rail by the door to help herself up the van steps. The baby's not due until July, but Christy is now *obviously* pregnant.

"Take this front seat, Christy," Mr. Rogers says. "It's the most comfortable seat in the van, besides mine."

The plan is to get to our motel by two, do a last minute practice of our debate material, and go to dinner at some little place Mr. Rogers knows about on Coronado Island.

There aren't really any rough spots, though. We all seriously want to go to nationals, and we all seriously have been working hard on our presentations.

We are on the freeway and singing kiddy camp songs by ten in the morning. We do "She'll Be Comin' 'Round the Mountain When She Comes," and "Old McDonald Had a Farm," complete with sound effects for the first hour or so, then Dashan starts us on "Ninety-nine Bottles of Beer on the Wall." That lasts until we're down to thirty-seven bottles of beer on the wall.

Mr. Rogers pulls to the side of the road and shuts off the ignition.

"I can't stand it! I'm not driving another inch unless you guys stop singing that stupid song!"

We sing down to twenty-six bottles of beer, sitting at the side of the road. Then I guess Trin decides it's time for us to move on because she starts "Down in the Valley." Hung and Dashan join in. They must still remember the harmonies from when choir did that number last year, because they sound really good together.

It's funny how a song, or a smell, or the warm sun on your shoulders, can take you back to another time. "Down in the Valley" does that to me. The first time I ever heard that song, Christy and I were sitting close, holding hands, in the auditorium. It was the choir's fall concert and Christy and I had only been hanging around together for a month or so. But when the combined choirs had sung the part that goes, "Angels in heaven, know I love you," we had squeezed hands and looked at each other in a way that we both knew meant something. After that, to the very end, one of us would say "Angels in heaven," and the other would know it meant "I love you," only more.

"Know I love you, dear, know I love you," they're singing now. "Angels in heaven, know I love you." I feel it, something lost, an emptiness in the pit of my stomach. I turn my face to the window and look out at patches of wildflowers blooming on the hills north of the freeway. I don't want to get back with Christy. What we had is past. But I steal a look at her and see that she too has turned her head toward the window next to her, so that no one can see her face. I wonder, can she still feel my hand in hers, as I can feel her hand in mine? Does she still know the taste of my lips, as I know hers?

"**L**unch time!" Mr. Rogers says.

We pull off the freeway and into a rest stop that over-looks the ocean. We buy sodas from a catering truck, then climb down steps which lead to picnic tables in the sand. The sun is bright, reflecting off the blue water. We've all brought sack lunches for the occasion. After we eat, Rogers brings out his ancient frisbee. He claims he went to a school that had a top-rated frisbee team. No football team, just a frisbee team. He says someday, when the world's a better place to live, we'll be sitting around on New Year's Day watching championship frisbee playoffs in the Rose Bowl, in all of the Bowls, instead of watching guys mutilate one another.

"Jeff!" he calls to me.

I jump to catch the frisbee Rogers has thrown my way, then throw it to Dashan. We take our shoes off and play around in the sand, all except Christy who sits watching, for about twenty minutes, then we get back on the road.

It's still dark out when I awaken in the Best Western motel in San Diego. In the bed across from me, Jeremy is sound asleep. I start with my Dramatic Interpretation piece, saying it in my head, reviewing gestures, reminding myself of the rules I've known by heart since my first tournament in the ninth grade. Then I review the facts for Policy Debate. What if I mess up? I won't mess up. I know it. But the competition is going to be so tough!

If it weren't for the scholarship, I could relax. Get to

nationals, don't get to nationals, no big deal. But tuition
and books paid, room and board paid—and Brooker University! From the pictures in the catalog it looks beautiful—brick buildings surrounded by huge trees. No smog.
No traffic. No earthquakes or drive-by shootings. I'll be a
college man, living in a dorm, totally on my own.

Jeremy says, "What're you doing over there, wrestling a
bear?"

It's getting lighter. I can see that he's sitting up in bed,
looking in my direction.

"What do you mean?" I ask.

"You! You're tossing and turning like you're in mortal
combat with a tyrannosaurus."

"Oh. Sorry. I guess I've been wrestling my speeches."

"Piece of cake," Jeremy says, lying back down and
turning away from me. "We've got all our facts and phrases
ready for Policy Debate, and your short story thing always
knocks their socks off. Relax."

Easy for him to say. It takes two hands to count Jeremy's
scholarship possibilities and one finger to count mine.

We meet in the school cafeteria at eight in the morning.
Everything here is shiny and clean. The walls are painted
with huge murals depicting California history—Cabrillo
sailing into San Diego Bay, Father Junípero Serra at the
San Diego Mission, a Gold Rush scene, the bridges at San
Francisco Bay. This place makes the Hamilton High cafeteria look like Skid Row in comparison.

Hundreds and hundreds of people are milling around,
getting set up. Dashan, Jeremy and Trin take their files of
reference materials over to the Extemp room. I don't know
how they do it. I need preparation time, practice time,
thinking time. Both of the events I compete in allow for
that. Even Policy Debate, where Jeremy and I have been
working as partners since our sophomore year, allows for
plenty of preparation. We have to be spontaneous and able

to respond to our opponent's arguments, whatever they come up with, but we know practically all there is to know on our subject when we go in there. Jeremy especially knows the facts—I'm good at coming up with the quick argument, though. We're a good team.

But in the Extemporaneous events, the debater gets three questions to choose from, like, say, "Can American political campaigns overcome recent practices of mudslinging?" or "Is the President of the United States a figurehead?" Then they get seven minutes to prepare for their speech, and seven to present it. They've got to have supporting facts, and they can't take any notes in with them. Sometimes I go watch those events, just to see Dashan or Jeremy in that kind of action. Those guys are always watching CNN, or saving articles for their fact files—in a way they're always preparing.

Everybody here has points in the National Forensics League. It's funny, when I first began winning in tournaments and I told my dad about my NFL rating, he got all excited. Great, I thought, he's finally proud of me and he's going to start paying attention. But it turned out he thought I was talking about football. When he realized the F in NFL stood for Forensics it was just one big yawn to him. But I don't care. Why should I care?

"Hey, J.B.!" I hear a voice screeching at me from across the cafeteria and I don't even have to look up to know who it is.

"Dawn!" I answer. Dawn and Delia are these two girls from Kennedy High School. They're partners in Policy Debate and Jeremy and I often compete against them.

"We're ready for you and Jeremy!" Dawn says, laughing.

"What room are you in for Policy?" I ask.

Neither of us is sure what our first event is, so we fight the crowd to look at the postings taped to the walls.

"Where's Jeremy?" she asks.

"In the Extemp room."

"So's Delia . . . Looks like we won't kick your butts for

another two hours," she says, pointing to the Policy Debate roster and laughing.

I hear Rogers' booming voice, "Hamilton Debaters, over here." He's motioning toward a table we've got staked out in the corner.

"Gotta go," I say, and go back to our table where I know we're going to get a pep talk which will exaggerate our skills and talents. We make fun of Rogers' talks sometimes, but I guess they work. I hope that's true today. I want to qualify for nationals more than anything else in the world. Well, almost more than anything else in the world, I think, glancing at Christy who is standing next to Trin. Absolutely more than anything else in the world, I want Christy not to be pregnant. But at least I've got a shot at nationals. I guess there's no way in hell, now, for Christy to not be pregnant. I don't want to think about it.

There's a break around one. Mr. Rogers has sent out for pizza and we've got an ice chest full of sodas.

"You're doing great!" he says. "Don't lose your concentration. Each round is important, but right now, the way things are going, we've got a good chance for several firsts."

We talk about our competition. Dashan says, "There's a girl, Ellie, I think her name is—does an amazing D.I. from *To Kill a Mockingbird.*"

"Everybody does something from *To Kill a Mockingbird,*" Hung says. "That's old stuff."

"Not the way she does it, it isn't. She scares me."

"Yeah, Ellie," Mr. Rogers says, taking a bite of pizza. "She's from up north, Susanville High School or something. She's good . . . Also, Kendall, from Palm Springs. But none of them are any better than you guys, at your best. Be your best, that's all."

About seven that evening, rosters are posted for the semi-finals. Jeremy, Trin and I have made it in two events, Dashan, Christy and Hung each made it in one. After checking the various rosters we gather back around our table, hugging each other and laughing.

"You guys are great!" Mr. Rogers says. If you can ever say someone's face is lit up with a smile, his is.

Somehow Jeremy and I got lucky and got a room with cable TV. All the other rooms just have plain old TV, so after dinner everyone piles on the bed and the floor in our room and we watch a movie, *Grand Canyon*. There's this scene where a yuppie-type woman is running through an expensive residential area and she hears a baby cry. She follows the sound and finds a baby lying on a blanket, on the grass behind some bushes.

"How could *anyone* leave their baby like that?" Christy says.

"I don't know," Dashan says. "Maybe the mom, or dad, or whoever, wanted it to have a better home than they could give it."

God! I want to kiss Dashan for saying that. Well . . . not really *kiss* him, but I'm glad he said it 'cause Christy listens to him. Maybe if everyone said that kind of thing to her she'd think seriously about adoption.

It turns out that *Grand Canyon* is a cool movie—very realistic about life in L.A. but also kind of reassuring about how nature is so big, and the universe is so vast, our problems are miniscule in comparison. The last scene is of the main characters looking out over the Grand Canyon.

"Awesome," Jeremy says. "We ought to go there on the way home."

"The way home? . . . You're nuts," Hung says.

"No. What would it be? Another two days—just swing by. It'd be inspiring."

Jeremy uses his best debate style to try to convince us we should "swing by" the Grand Canyon, but we all know it's just a fantasy, and slowly people start drifting back to their own rooms. "I don't care about this bunch of non-imaginative dullards," Jeremy says. "I'm going to see all the natural wonders of the world by the time I'm thirty, and I'm going to start with the Grand Canyon. Soon."

By mid-afternoon on Sunday, Jeremy and I are posted for Finals in Policy Debate, Dashan and I are posted for Finals in Dramatic Interpretation, and Trin is in for Oratory and Extemp. Christy and Hung are not posted for Finals.

"You've got plenty of time to get to nationals," Rogers tells them both. "You've done amazingly well as sophomores."

Hung stays to watch the finals but Christy says she's tired and goes back to the motel. After she leaves, Trin says, "I think it took guts for her to be here. I know teen pregnancy is supposedly reaching mammoth proportions, but you don't see a lot of pregnant girls at debate tournaments."

"One," Dashan says. "I counted."

Nobody looks my way while this conversation is taking place.

Ellie, from Susanville, is the first to speak in the D.I. finals. I see what they meant yesterday when Mr. Rogers and Dashan were talking about how good she was. Next is a guy who does a piece about AIDS, from a play called "Angels in America." He's going along great, and then he stops, mid-sentence. God. It's every debater's fear, that they'll lose it in the middle.

Come on, I think, rooting for him, as I'm sure the other competitors are, too. We all want to win, of course, but no one likes to see a guy lose it this way. He stands for what seems a long time, looking at some invisible spot on the back wall, then starts over, and completes his piece. He's good, but I know that lapse cost him the possibility of placing in this round—which is *the* round.

I'm next. I stand in front of the group, take several slow, deep breaths, and focus my concentration. By the second sentence of my introduction I get a feeling something like what I think runners get when their bodies start releasing endorphins. It's as if everything is smooth—the emphasis is right, the words and gestures are right.

When I speak the last line, "I was sixteen years old, and waiting for the next thing my father would tell me," I know I've done the best D.I. I've ever done. I may not win. Someone else may be better, but I did my best.

Dashan and I have taken first and second places, back and forth, all year long. When he stands to do his piece from *Roots,* I think this first place is probably his, if it's not Ellie's. Dashan is impressive as he delivers the words of the slave, Kunta Kinte, about being as a giant tree to his manchild, even in the midst of the terrible hardships of slavery. I watch the judges' faces but they're unreadable.

After the round we all wait in the cafeteria for results. Christy comes back around seven and waits with us. Hung and Trin play chess, moving their pieces as fast as nine-year-olds playing checkers. Jeremy and I play gin rummy, then stop mid-game when the judges come in.

They stand on a platform and we all hover around. Trin takes first place in Oratory and Jeremy takes first place in Extemp. Trin gets a third in Extemp, which in itself is not too shabby.

When the judge starts reading the D.I. results I hold my breath. I don't know why. I always do that when I hear results of an event I've competed in. The guy who forgot his lines is last, predictably. Then comes Kendall who did something from "The Crucible." So then it's down to me, Ellie and Dashan. When the judge calls Ellie's name for third place, Dashan and I link arms. Then Dashan's name, then me.

Trin throws her arms around me first, then we're all in a big group hug, including Mr. Rogers. In the mass of bodies I realize that I have my arm around Christy's shoulder. She looks up at me and says, "Congratulations, Jeff. You deserve it." She smiles, then turns to Dashan and plants a kiss on his cheek. "You're a winner, too," she says.

One of the great things about debate is that we all pull for each other. Dashan means it when he congratulates me and admires my first place trophy. Just like I meant it at the last tournament, where he took first and I took second. Same with Jeremy and Trin—they compete, but they root for each other, too.

I can hardly believe it when Jeremy and I take first place in Policy Debate. The two big Ds, Dawn and Delia, come running over and throw their arms around us.

"You won't have us to kick around next year," Dawn says, recognizing the fact that we're all seniors, and we'll be leaving this part of our lives behind.

In the van on the way home, Mr. Rogers tells Trin, me, and Jeremy that we'd better be saving our money for the trip to New Orleans because we've almost for certain qualified.

"Start listening to those jazz tapes, my man," Jeremy says, elbowing me in the ribs.

"It's not official until NFL does the numbers, but I'd bet my next paycheck you three are in."

Trin falls asleep with her head on my shoulder, while I watch the dark water break into white waves off to my left. I wonder if this means I'll be in Texas in the fall, and what will it be like to be a thousand miles from the Pacific Ocean. And what about Christy and the baby? I close my eyes, lean my head down on top of Trin's and start counting. If I count, I can't think about the baby.

CHAPTER

12

"**J**eff! Open this!"

My mom is standing in the driveway, waving an envelope at me as I get out of my car after work.

"I can't stand it," she says. "I wanted to open it myself."

I take the envelope from her. Return address: Office of Admissions, Brooker University, Brooker Springs, Texas.

"Open it! Open it!"

I hesitate. What if it doesn't say what I want it to say? Then I rip open the envelope and yank out the letter.

Dear Mr. Jeffrey Browning: We are pleased to inform you that you are the recipient of . . .

"I got it! I got it!" I drop my gym bag and grab Mom, lifting and twirling her around.

She's screaming, "Oh, my God. Oh, my God."

Stacy comes running across the street.

"What's wrong? What happened?"

I put Mom down and hand Stacy the letter.

"You got a scholarship?"

"Yes . . . Yes, yes, yes!" I am grinning so hard it hurts.

Mom is laughing and crying all at once. Stacy throws herself at me, nearly knocking me over.

"I'm happy for you, Jeff. But I'll miss you. Texas is a long way away," she says, stating the obvious.

"I'll be home for Christmas," I start singing, in imitation of Bing Crosby.

"But it won't be the same as seeing your beastly face on a daily basis."

Mom takes the letter from Stacy.

"I'm going to call Steve," she says, running into the house. She's back outside in a few minutes.

"Steve wants us to meet him at Barb and Edie's. He says this is an occasion to mark with a garbageburger."

"Great. I'm starving," I say.

"Me, too," Stacy says, "or is this only a family affair?"

"You're family, Stacy," Mom says. "Come with us."

I run in and wash up, then the three of us climb in my car and we drive down into the industrial area of Fifth Street. Steve is parked out front of Barb and Edie's, waiting in the car for us. He bear-hugs me when we meet at the door.

"I'm proud of you, Jeff," he says with a big smile. Then his face darkens with sadness, like it still does now and then. "God, I wish Janie were alive to see this. She thought you were the greatest kid around. Remember?"

"I remember," I say, thinking of Janie's quick smile and easy laugh.

We sit down at a round table near the back. Barb and Edie's is not the kind of place where you have to wait for a maitre d' to seat you. There are paper placemats on the red formica table, and a mural of Bridal Veil Falls on the side wall.

"What can I get for you?" Edie calls from the counter.

"Garbageburgers all around," Steve says, "Two orders of onion rings . . . what to drink?" he asks us, then relays the message, "Three Cokes and a Dr. Pepper."

"Regular or diet?"

"Regular," Steve says.

I've never seen either Edie or her partner, Barb, use an

order pad, no matter how many orders they're taking at
once. The other waitresses do, but never the bosses.

Steve reads my letter out loud while we're waiting for
our food, then hands it back to me.

"What a deal!" he says. "Tuition, books, room and board.
Boy, this plus the money from Grandma and your mom,
should have you sitting pretty. I wonder how you'll like
dorm life?"

We're talking about how part of the agreement is that I
will work on campus fifteen hours a week, when Barb
comes out from the back room and walks over to our table.
She's carrying a little kid.

"Hey, Shane!" she calls to the guy who's busing tables.
"Go put the stuff away from the delivery that just came in,
would you?"

Shane stops what he's doing and shuffles toward the
back. Barb shakes her head.

"If that guy wasn't Edie's nephew, he'd be out of here,"
she says, shifting the kid from one side to the other. Stacy
tries to hand the kid an onion ring, but she hides her face
in Barb's shoulder.

"I hear you folks are celebrating?" Barb says.

"Jeff's getting a scholarship to a college in Texas," my
mom says, beaming.

"Hey! The onion rings are on us," Barb says, laughing
her hoarse laugh. "No, that's great, though!"

Barb reaches over and ruffles my hair. "Got a brain
under there, huh?"

"I wouldn't jump to that conclusion," Stacy says, getting
a big laugh from everyone.

I'm feeling great—surrounded by some of my most
favorite people, an exciting, paid for, college life ahead of
me, eating my favorite food. Rolling in clover, as my
grandma would say. Then Barb says to me, "My daughter,
Emmy—remember Emmy? She went to Hamilton High."

I nod my head, even though I only sort of remember
Emmy. I think she graduated a couple of years ago.

"Well, Emmy was going away to college, too. But then this little gal changed things. Didn't you, Rosie?"

The little girl looks at Barb, smiles, and shakes her head.

"Yep. Emmy had plans to be the big college girl up north, away from home, living in a dormitory," Barb says, laughing that hoarse laugh again. "Now Rosie's her roommate and Emmy's taking classes at that glorified high school called Hamilton Heights City College," she says, then walks back to the counter, still carrying the little girl.

The mood at our table is not so light, now. I hardly ever talk about Christy's pregnancy to anyone. I guess I try to forget about it. There's nothing I can do. But always, somewhere under the surface of things, I'm aware that she's carrying a baby that's a part of me. And everyone at the table is aware of that, too, even if we don't talk about it. Well, I can't help it if she's going to have my baby. It's not my fault, and it's not going to ruin my life.

"Hey, Sis, you've got something to celebrate, too. Right?" Steve says, turning the attention away from me to Mom.

She smiles. "Yep. Karen Browning, girl nurse. Can you believe it, after all these years of trying to balance night school and work, and training sessions at the hospital?"

"Not to mention raising this hunk," Stacy says.

"When's graduation?" Steve asks.

"May 29th. You'd better all be saving that date for me."

"I wouldn't miss it for anything," Steve says.

"Me, either, Mommy K," Stacy says.

"We'll party hearty," I say.

Mom gives me a look, the kind that used to scare me when I was little. Ever since she had to come get me at the ranger station she acts like maybe I'm getting a big drinking problem. When I try to tell her I almost never have more than one beer, usually not even that, she gets this look on her face, like maybe so, maybe not. Between Christy being pregnant and me getting busted in the mountains, things aren't quite as easy between me and my mom as they were before. It's not like she's mad—just kind of edgy, like she could *get* mad any minute. I think it's a good thing I'll be going away to school in September.

"How about you, Stacy?" Steve asks. "What will you be doing after high school?"

"I don't know. I still want to be a vet, but I'm afraid it's too hard."

"Maybe you should try nursing," my mom says. "It's a shorter course, and there's always one or two patients in a ward who act like animals."

That gets us all playing the what should Stacy be when she grows up game—stuff with animals that doesn't require too much school. Work for the Humane Society, or at a zoo, or at the race track, or open her own pet-sitting business, or grooming shop.

"Okay, okay," Stacy says. "I get the picture. You want me to have a life—a plan. I'll give it some serious thought," she says, striking the classic "Thinker" pose.

After dinner Stacy and I sit on the curb in front of my house and talk for a long time.

"Everything will be different next year," she says.

"It's different every year," I tell her.

She knuckle-punches me on the arm before I have time to flex.

"I'm serious," she says. "All of our friends will be going all different directions. You're going to be in Texas. Who's going to insult me when you're gone?"

"Someone will turn up."

"I'm scared," she says.

"Of what?"

"I don't know. Growing up, I guess. My mom's already telling me if I don't go to school next year I've got to get a full-time job, and pay room and board. Can you believe it?"

"Sounds fair to me," I say.

"Oh, yeah, easy for you to say, big scholarship dude.

You're not paying room and board anywhere!"

She punches me again. I punch her back. Not mean or anything, just enough to let her know she can't walk all over me. We argue some more, then she asks, "What about God?"

"What about God?" I repeat.

"You know, is there or isn't there?"

That's how our conversations go—from one extreme to the other. I don't know about God and neither does Stacy, but it's been a favorite subject with us for a long time.

"How could God kill Janie with breast cancer?" I ask my standard question. When Janie died, first I was mad at God, and then I thought maybe there was no such thing.

"Maybe He wanted her in heaven," Stacy says.

"But why punish Uncle Steve?"

"Maybe he did something really bad that we don't know about."

"That's bullshit," I say. "I think if there is a god, he just got us all started and forgot about us."

Then I see this bright shining shooting star that streaks across the whole sky.

"Wow!" Stacy says. "Did you see that?" She laughs. "I think God was telling us something."

"Coincidence," I say. But it's kind of weird. Like maybe it was a special sign or something. It was the brightest shooting star I've ever seen.

13

Fourth period, a student aide comes in and hands a summons to Mrs. Rosenbloom. It's the third summons already and we're not even halfway through the class. She sighs. "I swear, we'll never get finished discussing Herman Melville with all these interruptions."

She reads the summons, then calls my name.

"Mrs. Gould wants to see you in the nurse's office."

"Why?" I ask.

"Go see," she says. "I don't know. My specialty is Melville, not mind-reading."

I jam my stuff in my backpack and leave. I walk past the principal's office, past the guidance center, to the health center, where I take a seat on a cold metal chair. Across from me, some guy is curled up sleeping on a cot sort of like the one I slept on when I stayed at Steve's, except I didn't have to use a paper cover on my pillow. It's not long before a short, stocky woman opens the door to her private office.

"Jeff Browning?" she asks.

I stand and hand her my summons.

"Come in," she says.

I follow her into the office. It smells of rubbing alcohol,

like the nurse's office at my old elementary school.

"Have a seat," she says.

There are posters on every wall—institutional style stuff with broad black letters warning **Wash Hands After Using the Toilet**, and the classic fried egg **This Is Your Brain on Drugs**, and one that says **No Glove, No Love** with a picture of a girl holding a condom at arm's length.

I remember Mrs. Gould from an AIDS talk she did in our Health and Safety class last year. She was funny and to the point, and she gave us plenty to think about.

"So Jeff, I talked with your girlfriend yesterday," she says.

"I don't have a girlfriend."

"Oh, really?" she says, eyebrows raised, voice going cold. "Then I talked with the girl you got pregnant. Do you like that description better? Christina Calderon? Remember her? Or do you have so many other pregnant non-girlfriends running around that you can't keep track?"

"It's not like that," I say.

"Then tell me. How is it?"

I don't know what I'm supposed to say. I liked Mrs. Gould when she talked to our class, but now she seems nosy and grouchy. Why should I talk to her? Do I have to?

"Well?" she says.

"Well . . . Christy used to be my girlfriend."

"She tells me you're the father of her unborn baby, and now you don't want to take any responsibility for it. Is that true?"

"Sort of. But did she tell you that she pretended to be on the pill and she wasn't? It's not *my* fault."

"Maybe you'll want to drop your child a line someday and tell him it's not your fault he, or she, doesn't have a dad who cares. I'm sure that will make the little tyke feel much better," Mrs. Gould says, oozing sarcasm.

"Can I go back to class now?" I ask, standing up.

"No," she says, motioning for me to sit back down. She looks at me intently, appraising me, it seems.

"Maybe we got off to a bad start, Jeff. Let me start over. Okay?"

"Okay." What else can I say?

"I've just finished getting Christina set up for the Teen Mothers Program. She'll be going to school there, starting Monday. Teenagers don't always understand what's going on with their bodies, or the necessity of getting early medical attention, or how to go about getting certain benefits. The Teen Mothers Program can help with that, as well as help her keep up academically."

"What about debate?" I ask.

"She can still take afternoon classes on this campus, if she can get her own transportation . . . But what I want to talk to you about is the weekly meeting with the dads over at the teen moms' campus. I think it's important the dads be involved too, don't you?"

"I guess. If they want to be dads. *I* don't want to be a dad."

"Well . . ." Mrs. Gould says. "Where do you fit into this picture?"

"I don't! I'm sorry I ever believed she was on the pill and stopped using condoms. I'm going away to college in September. I wanted her to get an abortion, but no, she wouldn't do it. And now I'm the bad guy because *I* won't take responsibility. What about Christy saying she was on the pill and then not taking it? Why isn't everyone bagging on her? Her friends won't even talk to me. Not that I care, I don't like her friends anyway . . ." I don't know why I'm going on and on, because, like I said earlier, I hardly ever talk to anyone about Christy being pregnant.

Then I surprise myself by saying what I've been trying not to think about all along. "I really don't want some little kid running around without a dad—some little kid of mine."

God. Now I've said it, I feel like crying.

Mrs. Gould gives me another of those appraising looks. "You're caught between a rock and a hard place."

I nod. "What am I supposed to do?"

"I don't have any answers for you. I called you in to talk with you about rights and responsibilities, and to strongly suggest you involve yourself in the after-school teen dad's program. Too often no one pays much attention to teen dads, except to criticize. I always try to have a conference or two along the way, if I can find out who they are. Of course, the dads aren't as easy to spot," she says with a laugh.

Mrs. Gould tells me I have a right to regular visits with the baby, and to total custody under certain circumstances. Christy can't put the baby up for adoption without my consent.

"But I want her to put the baby up for adoption," I say. "That way it would have good parents who really want it, and we could get on with our lives."

"That's what you say now, but people sometimes change their minds after the baby gets here."

"I won't."

"Well, just as Christy can't give the baby up without your consent, you can't force her to give it up either. But to make sure all of your rights as a father are protected, it's important for you to get to the hospital when the baby is born, so you can be sure your name gets put on the birth certificate. That helps protect your paternity rights."

"I don't want to think about this stuff," I say.

"But it's stupid to hide your head in the sand. No offense intended, but haven't you been stupid enough already?"

"I guess," I say, smiling.

"Okay. Another thing teen dads need to know is that just because they're kids doesn't let them off the financial hook."

"What do you mean?"

"I mean that it's up to you to help support your child financially. That's not just my idea. That's the law. You're working. Right?"

"Right."

"Part of each paycheck needs to go to the support of

your kid."

I groan.

"Isn't that fair?"

"It's not fair that Christy got pregnant!"

"But we're talking about a child now. Your child. Isn't that fair for the child?"

"Shit!" I say, forgetting I'm with a teacher-type. She seems not to notice.

"Yep," she says. "Nothing easy about being between a rock and a hard place. Like it or not, though, that's where you are. It might be easier if you were on speaking terms with Christina."

"Maybe," I say. But that's something else I don't want to think about.

For the rest of the school day, I have trouble concentrating in my classes. Why does life have to be so complicated?

As if my talk with the nurse hadn't stirred up enough troubled feelings, my dad is waiting for me when I get home from school. He's sitting in front of my house, in a new Jeep, with a personalized license plate. H-A-N-K-4-0, it says. What is *he* doing here? He honks and waves as I pull into my driveway. I wish I could disappear. He walks up the driveway to meet me as I get out of my car.

"Hey, Jeffie," he says, all smiles.

"Hi, Dad."

He gives me a big hug. I stand, arms at my side, wondering why now.

"I was thinking about you today—thought I'd take a chance and drop by, see if I could catch you after school. I couldn't wait to show my main man this new toy of mine," he says.

Right. That's why the Jeep has personalized license plates firmly attached to both bumpers. It's like he still thinks I'm some stupid little kid. Everyone knows it takes at least two months to get California plates on a new car.

But I let him think what he thinks. If he wants to pretend he just drove his car off the showroom floor and straight to my place, let him pretend. It's nothing to me one way or the other.

He puts his arm around my shoulders and walks me toward the Jeep. "Here, get in. I'll take you for a ride."

"I've got to get to work pretty soon," I say.

"Okay, just around the block."

I climb into the car. It still smells new.

"What do you think? Nice, huh? CD player, leather interior," he says, rubbing his hand along the back of my seat. "And check this out." He points to a digital display over the middle of the windshield. "What do you want to know? Temperature? Direction?" He presses a button and the display says NW 72 degrees. "Great, huh?"

I think of the Honda my mom's been driving for twelve years. We're heading toward the freeway.

"Dad," I say. "This is more than around the block. I have to be at work in thirty minutes and I've got to change clothes before I go."

I glance over at him. It's creepy, like looking at an older version of me. Brown eyes. Brown hair. High forehead. Dimple in the chin. Pointy teeth to the side of the front ones. Our hands are alike, too. We both have long fingers, and our little fingers turn inward—not just a little either—they're bent big-time. Crooked as a dog's hind leg is my grandma's description. No one else in the world has pinkies like we do.

When I was little I loved it when people said how much I looked like my dad. But then when I realized what a butthead he was, I wanted to dye my hair black, get my dimple filled and have my fingers straightened.

"Still working at the gym?"

"Yeah. I'm assistant manager now."

"You shouldn't have given up football."

I just look at him. Who is he to be telling me what I should and shouldn't do?

"Do you miss coming out to the games and watching me play?" I say, sarcastically.

His salesman smile fades. "I know, Jeffie. Turning forty caused me to think about my life. Little Donny, he's seven now, you know. He reminds me of you sometimes, and I feel bad that I didn't pay more attention to you when you were a kid."

I can't look at him.

"So, anyway," he goes on, "I was thinking maybe we'd pile in the Cherokee and go camping over the long Memorial Day weekend. Just you and me and Donnie. Give you a chance to know your brother better . . ."

My brother! That's a laugh. I've seen him four times in my whole life. I guess technically he's my half-brother, but whenever anyone asks me if I have brothers or sisters, I always say no. I can't think of a total stranger as my brother.

"Mom's graduating from nursing school that Saturday. It's a big deal," I say.

"She'd understand," he says. "It'll be fun, Jeffie. You can be with your mom any time. We haven't been camping together since you were about four years old. Remember when we camped down at Doheny Beach?"

I remember. He'd carried me on his shoulders out in the ocean, Mom yelling at him to not go out so far. I'd felt safe though, gripping his hair, laughing when he dunked me up and down. He'd built a fire in the evening and we roasted weinies. And then, not long after, he was gone.

"Remember how much fun we had in the water, you on my shoulders?" he says.

"No," I lie.

We pull up in front of the house, and it suddenly looks shabby to me. The paint is peeling around the front windows, and the driveway is all cracked. I know my dad lives in a fancy new townhouse over in Santa Monica, with his new family.

I want out of the car, but I can't find the door handle at

first.

"At least think about the Memorial weekend trip, would you? I know I screwed up, Jeffie."

I find the handle.

"Everyone calls me Jeff," I say. I get out and walk up the driveway to my back door. I don't look back.

After I've officially finished my shift at the Fitness Club, I get on a treadmill. I run seven miles an hour for forty minutes. Usually I only stay on the treadmill for twenty minutes. I guess I'm running off the conversation with Mrs. Gould, and the visit from my dad, trying to sweat everything out of my system. Too bad it's not that easy.

How could my dad just show up like that and expect to be all buddy-buddy? Usually I see him once or twice a year, near Christmas and maybe near my birthday. He takes me someplace for pizza, I open my gift, and he takes me back home. This year for my birthday he sent a check for twenty-five dollars and a card that said Happy Birthday Son on it. What had I expected for my eighteenth birthday, anyway? Pony rides and balloons?

Now and then he calls, but usually it's just to tell my mom that his check may be a little late. The last phone call he made he said hi to me, then talked to my mom and reminded her that his child support responsibilities end as soon as I finish high school.

Then he turns forty, feels guilty, and decides a camping weekend in his Yuppiemobile will take care of all those Saturdays when something else came up. I'm sorry, big H-A-N-K-4-0. I think it's not that easy.

14

The people I've known all my life show up at my mom's graduation. We take up a whole row of seats in the Hamilton Heights Community College auditorium. Next to me is Steve, then Stacy, then my mom's best friend May, and May's kids, Dayton and Norma, and some other people from the real estate office where my mom worked until just this week, when she started work at the hospital.

Even my grandma from Florida is here. She's going to stay three weeks, through my graduation, then go back home.

This will be the first summer since I was five that I won't visit my grandma in Florida. I'm going to work full-time at the Club, overtime if I can, and try to save a lot of money, so maybe I can get by without working extra hours my first semester at Brooker University. Even though my scholarship will pay for a lot, I'll still have a bunch of general expenses, like for my car and clothes. I'm still not thinking about what Mrs. Gould told me, about being legally responsible for child support.

I can tell by the way my grandmother looks at me that my mom's told her about Christy being pregnant. Every time I walk into a room where just Grandma is sitting, I'm afraid she's going to start asking a bunch of questions. I know she will, sooner or later.

Right now, a man in a purple robe with some kind of a long scarf around his neck is talking about the importance of nursing all through history. I try to concentrate, but he's speaking in a monotone—not really speaking either, mostly reading. He could stand a little coaching from Mr. Rogers. This guy wouldn't make it to the second round at a debate tournament.

There are thirty-two nursing graduates sitting on the stage, facing us. Five of them are men. Several of the women are gray haired, but some look like they're about my age. One sort of reminds me of Christy. That's all I need to be distracted from Dr. What's-his-name's droning speech.

I don't admit this to anyone, but sometimes I miss Christy very much. I see a lot more of Jeremy and Benny, like I wanted to, but to tell the truth, I get sort of tired of playing pool and horsing around. It's hard to talk seriously with guys. With Christy, I could tell her anything and know she'd understand, but with Jeremy and Benny, I end up hiding my feelings, laughing, and pretending nothing is important to me.

And, to tell the truth, I miss Christy loving me. I miss the feel of her in my arms, and the look in her eyes when we would start getting sexy. I miss her midnight phone calls, and her laugh. I miss her laugh a lot. Not that I want to get back with her—so much has changed.

And I *don't* miss having to always be bolstering her spirits, or comforting her because of some big fight at home. But sometimes, late at night, when everything's quiet, I remember how things used to be with Christy, and I feel all empty inside.

I took that girl, Kelly, from my English class, out to a movie last Friday night. After, we walked around Old Town for a while, then we stopped at Johnny Rockets for a giant serving of onion rings. It was okay. Kelly's a nice person and she's sort of cute. But her hand felt strange in mine. I kissed her goodnight when I took her home, hoping to feel something. All I felt was wrong.

"**K**aren Browning," the voice calls over the microphone.

I'm so busy thinking about myself, I practically miss seeing my mom walk across the stage. Everyone in my row jumps up when they call Mom's name. We clap and whistle—Stacy whistles the loudest of all.

We watch Mom move her tassle from the left to the right side, then sit back down. Most of the graduates have their own cheering section, and I feel sorry for the guy who only gets light, polite applause from the audience.

After the diplomas are handed out, the head of the nursing department, Dr. Mendoza, walks back up to the microphone. I hope she doesn't talk long. We're all going out for Thai food after this and I'm starving.

Dr. Mendoza is saying how proud she is to present this award, blah, blah, blah, and I'm thinking hurry up, hurry up, when she says, ". . . to Karen Browning, for academic achievement and practical expertise in the pursuit of nursing, the Dr. Eleanor Bunche Award for Excellence."

We're all on our feet now, whistling and yelling. Steve lifts Grandma up and kisses her. I can't believe it! I'm still standing, clapping, when Stacy tugs at my jacket and pulls me down in my seat.

My mom is standing next to Dr. Mendoza, who is saying, ". . . this woman had a dream of being a nurse. As often happens, life changed her mind for a while. She worked in a business capacity for many years, supporting herself and her young son, and then, as he approached adulthood, she entered the nursing school here at Hamilton Heights Community College. She was an excellent student from the beginning. But when she started her hospital internship, it became obvious what truly fine nursing material she was . . ."

Dr. Mendoza goes on and on about my mom. It's funny,

I knew she'd wanted to be a nurse from the beginning, but I'd never thought much one way or the other about any of that stuff. She was just my mom, always there to pick me up after school, arranging her real estate hours around my schedule.

When I was younger and she had to show houses on weekends, she saw to it that I had something fun to do, with Steve and Janie, or with May. She watched over my homework every night and went to all of the parent conferences and did the Little League and AYSO thing. She was a mom.

Steve's reserved the big round table near the back of the room at Flavors of Bangkok. People have brought cards and presents for my mom. Steve orders champagne and practically everyone proposes toasts. My mom is the absolute center of attention.

One of the men from Mom's graduating class, Douglas, has joined us for dinner. He's telling a story about how mom confronted this old, stubborn doctor who was about to release a diabetic patient with a very bad foot infection—something that needed extensive hospital treatment. She'd told the doctor that the infection was worse, not better. He'd insisted it was better, said that was obvious from the blood tests, and essentially told her to butt out.

"Karen waited in the patient's room until the doctor made his rounds. When he got there, she lifted the sheet and exposed this terribly infected foot and asked him how that compared with the blood tests. He called her out of the room, fuming!"

"I thought I was going to be kicked out of the program, then and there," Mom says.

"But it all worked out," Douglas continues. "The patient got the treatment he needed, and Karen actually won the respect of that crusty old doctor."

Mom and Douglas click glasses and laugh. What . . . ?

What is in that look? As I said before, my mom is just my mom to me. I don't think she has much of a private life. But, maybe?

In comparison to my mom's graduation, mine is dull. Seven hundred and twelve seniors in red and white caps and gowns sitting on risers out on the football field behind the superintendent of schools, who could also benefit from some coaching from Mr. Rogers.

Then the dean stands up and honors scholarship winners. Dashan's name is called three times and so is Jeremy's. I'm happy with my one mention, for the scholarship to Brooker University. When my name is called, I hear mom, Steve, and my grandma cheering above the other voices.

Finally, after talking about what a wonderful education Hamilton High offers the youth of our community, etc., etc., etc., Mr. Hill, the principal, begins calling names. We walk forward, one after the other, just the way we practiced earlier in the day. But there are so many of us it's like a parade with interchangeable people. We don't even get handed our real diplomas—it's all just pretend. Finally it's over and we pour off the risers to find family and friends in the audience. After hugs and kisses, I get my picture taken with my mom and Grandma and Steve.

My grandma leaves for Florida first thing in the morning. She hugs me tight.

"I'm so proud of you, Jeff," she says. "Don't forget our little talk."

"I won't, Grandma," I say. Really, our little talk consisted of her telling me how she had a friend in high school who committed suicide because the boy who got her pregnant wouldn't marry her. I don't know exactly why she told me that, but I listened because she's my grandma.

"Have a good trip," I tell her, hugging her again. Then I hurry over to the place where I turn in my rented cap and gown. From there I go out to the parking lot where the buses for Grad Night at Disneyland sit waiting.

The graduating debaters, Jeremy, Dashan, Trin, Patrick, Cassie and all the rest, will ride on the first bus together. We've got it all planned. Whoever gets there first will save a section of seats for the whole group, then we'll all hang out together at Disneyland. It's probably the last time we'll all be together. Jeremy and Trin and I are going to the national tournament in New Orleans nine days from now. Cool. I've already got my ticket packed in my book bag at home. But that's just the three of us, not the whole group of debate seniors who've been together these past four years.

All of those trips to tournaments, urging each other on, cheering each other up when we've just missed a trophy— over. It seems impossible that my time at Hamilton High has ended.

Jeremy is already in line at the first bus. As I make my way through the crowd, I'm surprised to see Christy's dad drop her off at the other end of the parking lot. Only grads and their dates get to attend Grad Night, and Christy's not a grad. Then I see Dashan walking to meet her. He takes her by the hand and walks over toward where the first bus is parked. I can't believe it! She's eight months pregnant and on a date? I turn and walk away, back toward the fourth bus in line. No way do I want to end up on the same bus with them.

Now I wish I'd invited Kelly to be my date. She'd kind of hinted around, but I didn't take the hint. I wanted to be on my own with my friends. I didn't want to have to be there with just one person. But I guess I won't be hanging out with the debaters now. I sneak a look back to the line at the first bus. Dashan has his arm around Christy. I don't get it!

I see Stacy standing by the music building and walk to meet her, but just then Frankie shows up and throws a big, passionate kiss on her, so I turn away from them, too. I'm feeling like the total Lone Ranger when I hear Benny calling to me.

"Hey! J.B.! Over here!"

What a relief. I hate standing around alone, staring at my kneecaps and doing a great imitation of a nerd. I walk over to Benny's car and greet him. Three other guys, John, Mark and Raymond, are standing by Benny's car.

"How's it going?" Mark says, extending his hand. I hardly recognize these guys, I'm so used to seeing them all dressed out in baggies. But Disneyland has a strict dress code and we've all paid big bucks for this night. No one wants to be turned away at the gate.

I don't have a problem with these guys, and I think my mom's sort of paranoid for telling me to stay away from them. I guess John is kind of hard core—he's on probation for something, but I don't hold that against him. Mark and Raymond and I played AYSO together. They're all pretty smart guys, but not in a way that any teacher would ever notice.

"Thirsty?" Benny says, reaching into a little Playmate ice chest on the floor of his car. He pulls out a can of beer and slips it into a plastic container that makes it look like a can of Seven-Up.

"No thanks, Benny," I say.

Mark, who's standing next to me, says, "You better take it, Homes. It's going to be a long time between brews."

"I can last," I say.

"More for me," Benny says, taking a long swig from the can he's just offered me.

"Hey, didja see Christy?" Ben asks.

I look at him carefully, wondering how much he's had to drink. He's sort of weaving back and forth, and his eyes look kind of glassy.

"Yeah, I saw her," I say.

"She's with that black scholarship guy," he says, laughing. "She's big bellied with your baby and she's holding hands with a nigger."

"She's with *Dashan*," I say, feeling my face grow hot. I

hate that nigger talk. Once, just before Christmas, Dashan and I went to the mall to get something for our moms. We're in this fancy department store, and I notice there's this security-type person sort of following us around. It made me feel really self-conscious but Dashan said he was used to it. You get used to that stuff if you're a black guy, he said. I don't understand why people think the way they do.

Benny says, "Want to fuck the nigger up?"

Now I know he's drunk. Benny says some really stupid things sometimes, but he's not racist, or mean. At least, not when he's sober.

"Don't be stupid, Ben," I say.

"Well, then, want us to fuck him up for you?" he says, gesturing toward the others.

"God, Benny. Stop talking crazy," I say.

"Come on," he says, taking off in the direction of Dashan and Christy. Mark and I run after him and grab him.

"Calm down," Mark says.

Benny pulls away from Mark but I manage to grab his other arm and hold on tight.

"Lemme go," he says, trying to squirm away.

"No. Benny. Stop acting crazy. Look," I say, "now you've got the narcs watching us."

It's true, Joe and Rochelle are leaning against the back of the last bus, walkie-talkies in hand, looking in our direction. Mark and I get Benny turned around and walk him back to his car. We try to be all casual about it. John and Raymond, always cool, are leaning against the car, watching us as if we were on TV instead of part of their lives.

I can tell by Benny's jerking movements as he tries to get free of my grip that he is totally bombed. I see a couple of teachers standing by the first bus, writing names on a clipboard and checking student IDs as they let the kids board. I hope no one looks very closely at Benny when it's his turn to get on a bus. I guess Mark must be thinking the same thing, because he tells Ben, "Cool it, or they won't even let your ass on the bus."

"I don't care!" Ben says. "I don't care about this phony-ass grad night shit anyway. I didn't even graduate so why should I give a shit! Damn Garner, anyway!"

Now I get it. Garner's Benny's history teacher.

"Hey, don't sweat it," John says. "There's always summer school. That's what I'm doing."

"Yeah, but I turned my work in and everything. Just 'cause it's late . . ."

Benny leans back against the car. We stand around for a while, talking of nothing, then notice that they're boarding the last bus.

"Come on, Ben," I say.

We all walk toward the bus, Benny between me and John. The two teachers who are checking people on don't seem to notice that Benny's not quite with it.

I'm the last in line, right behind Benny. Mark is in front of him and when he finds a seat he motions to Benny to take it. John and Mark and Raymond find seats near the back of the bus, but there's nothing left for me. I sit in the aisle at the back, next to Mark, but after the bus driver checks things out and counts heads, he turns to the teacher with the clipboard.

"We've got one too many kids on this bus."

"Does it matter?" she asks.

"Yep. It's the law. We don't move until one kid gets off this bus. Who was last on?"

She checks her clipboard and calls my name. God, I hate this. No one can get in unless they arrive on an official grad night bus. It's like being in elementary school again, all crowded together and being bossed around by a bus driver. I get up and walk to the front.

The bus driver is involved in conversation on his two-way radio.

"Nope. One too many. You got any room left? . . . How about Bob?"

He turns to me. "Don't worry, one of these buses has an

empty seat or two."

"Doreen? Hey, listen, you got room for one more on your bus? . . . Okay. Thanks."

He looks at me again. "Okay, kid. There's room on the number one bus. Run on up there so we can get this show on the road."

Just my luck. The bus I most want to avoid is the one I end up on. Not only that, but the vacant seat is in front of Trin and Patrick, across from Christy and Dashan.

Patrick pats me on the back.

"We wondered where you were," he says.

"Yeah. We almost sent out a search party," Trin says.

Dashan reaches across the aisle to shake hands. "Congratulations on your scholarship," he says, smiling.

I shake his hand. "You too, you scored big," I say, immediately regretting my choice of words. I don't look at Christy.

15

By the time we've gone five miles Trin has us singing the stuff we've always sung on our way to tournaments. I feel less awkward than when I first got on the bus. Everything along the 605 Freeway looks better at night, illuminated by headlights and street lights. The rock quarry, the rundown houses, the graffiti covering freeway walls, all have a pleasant glow, not like the dulled images of smog-filtered sunlit afternoons.

I remember looking down on the 210 Freeway from the place in the mountains where Jeremy and Benny and I had gone just after I'd found out Christy was pregnant. I wonder if there's some guy up on some hill looking down on us now, watching the pattern of moving lights, wondering about the pattern of his life.

Somewhere behind me I hear a bunch of people groan, and then Jeremy's voice, "No. Come on. This is really funny. It's a knick-knack Patty Wack, give the frog a loan."

"God, Jeremy," I yell back to him. "I suppose you're going to be telling that joke in the student lounge at Yale!"

"It's funny!" he yells back.

There's another mass groan.

"Okay, try this one then," Jeremy says.

I lean my head against the back of the seat and close my eyes. I feel the rumble of the rolling bus, mixed with the droning of Jeremy's voice as he tells another of his long jokes. I hear Trin telling Patrick about taking her dog to obedience training school and I hear Dashan telling Christy about how he's going to room with his brother at Berkeley. All of these voices, the voices I've been hearing around me for four years, listening to speeches, over the telephone, in class discussions, in the clamor of Hamilton's hallways, soon will be beyond the reach of my hearing. I let them float over me, surround me. I drink them in, knowing they soon will be lost to me. Usually I'm not sentimental, but right now I could almost cry.

Another groan, indicating Jeremy has delivered the punch line. I smile. Still with closed eyes, I try to imagine myself at Brooker University, in the dining hall, sitting under one of the tall pine trees in the main quad, just being there. It's going to be so great. I'll miss my old friends, and Mr. Rogers, and my mom and Steve, but I'll be getting a whole new life, all on my own.

It's nearly eleven when our buses arrive at Disneyland. There must be thousands of schools here, buses even from Nevada and Arizona, two from Oregon. And I thought *we* had a long ride.

Jeremy catches up to me as I step off the bus.

"We're all starting off at Star Tours, before the place gets too crowded," he says.

"I didn't know Christy would be here," I say.

"So? It's a free country. Come on. You should be relieved that someone's taken her off your hands. You want to be free, right?"

"Right," I say, walking along beside Jeremy.

A crowd has gathered around one of our buses and we stop to see what's happening. Four burly security guys are walking someone over to a Disneyland security car. I get a glimpse of the guy's jacket.

"Shit. It's Benny," I tell Jeremy.

I spot Mark in the crowd and we walk over to talk to him.

"What happened?" I ask.

"Oh, man, that sucks."

"What?"

"On the way down, on the bus, Benny had a beer can tucked inside his jacket and he was drinking from it with this extra-long straw. We were all laughing at him. It was just a joke. Then all of a sudden that narc Rochelle came out of nowhere. She ripped open Benny's jacket and grabbed the beer can."

"Stupid Benny," I say.

"Anyway, Rochelle took the beer can up to the front of the bus, and then it looked like they were having a big conference. Then Benny started yelling about how she stole his beer. So then the bus driver pulled over to the side of the freeway. Rochelle made Benny trade places with this schoolboy guy who'd been sitting next to her."

"What's going to happen now?" Jeremy asks.

"I don't know. As soon as I saw the driver talking into his two-way radio, I knew security would be waiting. It sucks. Benny paid all that money for his ticket and now he's probably going to spend grad night locked up in that little holding-tank place they've got down on Main Street, waiting for his parents to come get him."

I watch the black and white car drive off with Benny in it, feeling sorry for him but knowing there is nothing I can do. Jeremy and I start walking toward the gates.

"Benny acts really stupid sometimes," Jeremy says.

"Maybe it's not an act," I say. "Did you know he didn't graduate?"

"No. History?"

I nod my head. At the gate we have to take off our jackets, turn our pockets inside out, and let some old guy who's probably a pervert pat us down. Finally they let us in and we go directly to Star Tours.

The rest of the debate group is already there, singing "Yo ho, yo ho, a pirate's life for me . . ." I don't know why everyone is singing the song from the Pirates of the Caribbean when they're in the Star Tours line. It's probably ditzy Trin's idea.

Dashan is in line with everyone else, but Christy is sitting on one of the benches in front. As the line moves forward I see a sign that says no one with heart trouble, or high blood pressure, or who is pregnant, is allowed on Star Tours. I guess that's why Christy is sitting this one out.

At the last minute, just as it's my turn to move inside, I step out of line and go back to where Christy is sitting. When I get there I don't know what to say, so I just sit down next to her. She looks at me, then looks away.

"Christy . . ."

She sits looking at the little white twinkly lights.

"What's with you and Dashan?" I say. It doesn't come out right. But at least she looks at me.

"What do you care?"

"I'm trying to be friendly," I tell her. "I don't like that we can't even talk to each other anymore."

She turns her attention back to the lights, then says, "Dashan and I are mostly friends. He's there for me. Not like some other people I know."

Now it's my turn to stare at the lights.

"He takes me to the doctor. He picks me up at Teen Moms every day so I can still be in debate and still be an aide in the Hearing Impaired program."

"Oh, so he's like your chauffeur?"

Now she turns to look at me. "No, he's not like my chauffeur. He's like someone who cares, and who's not afraid to go out of his way to help a friend . . . You couldn't even be bothered to hear your own baby's heartbeat, but Dashan has.

"Dashan puts his hand on my stomach and feels your baby kick. Dashan's seen the sonogram and knows whether your baby is a girl or a boy. You don't even know that much."

Christy gets up and walks over to where our group is

leaving Star Tours. Dashan turns and walks to meet her.

"You doin' okay?" he asks, taking her hand.

There's that lonely, empty feeling again. What's wrong with me, anyway? I'm glad we broke up, so why should I still miss her?

I talk Jeremy into taking the train ride that circles the park. I want to get away from the debate group for awhile. As soon as the train enters the "Grand Canyon" area, Jeremy starts in on how he's going to see all the wonders of the world before he's thirty.

"Starting with the *real* Grand Canyon—not this phony Disneyland stuff."

But then he gets all into the Disneyland version—what kind of materials they used to make the dinosaurs in the big picture dioramas, how they got the color on the canyon walls, what they did to make the vegetation look so real. That's okay. I need a distraction after my attempt to talk with Christy. I guess I thought she'd be happy to talk with me again. I guess I was wrong. Oh well.

I don't even know why I tried to talk with her. It just seems so strange, that once we'd been so close and now we don't even say hi. I wish I could at least say hi to her when I see her at school. Not that I'll be seeing her at school anymore.

"Hey, you're not listening," Jeremy says.

"No. What?"

"The guys who put this stuff together were as scientifically advanced as the guys who did the first moon rocket."

"Whatever you say, J.J.," I tell him.

As soon as we get off the train in Fantasyland we hear this screeching.

"Jeremy! Jeffrey! The two Big Js!"

It's Delia and Dawn, from the Kennedy debate team.

"The two Big Ds!" Jeremy yells back.

We decide to ride Thunder Mountain with them, then end up walking around with them, going from ride to ride. We sort of pair up, Jeremy with Delia and me with Dawn.

It's nothing, but the next time we see Christy and Dashan I reach for Dawn's hand.

It's nearly three in the morning and I'm dragging. Dawn and Delia went back to meet some friends from Kennedy and Jeremy and I are standing in line with the rest of the debate group, waiting to get on "It's a Small World." Christy is in line, too. I guess this little-kid boat ride is safe.

I'm half asleep, floating past the singing Chinese dolls, when a scream pierces *my* small world. I look to the front of the boat and see Dashan and Trin hovering over Christy.

"What is it? What is it?" I hear him asking, but I can't hear her answer. I can see that she is covering her face with her hands and I think she is crying. I climb over two seats, and the people in them, to get closer.

"Is she okay?" I ask Dashan.

"I don't think so," he says.

She doesn't look up but keeps her face covered.

"I think something's happened," Trin says. "Like . . . I don't know. Something scared her."

"Christy. Christy," I say, but she won't answer, just keeps her head down, crying in strange little gasps.

We are near the end of the ride. I jump out onto a narrow ledge and run down to where the attendants are helping people off the boats.

"We need help!" I say. "Fast."

One of the guys in a Disneyland uniform takes me aside. "What's wrong?"

"My girlfriend. She's pregnant and something's happened. I don't know what. Get a doctor!"

By this time the boat Christy is in has come to a stop. Dashan is trying to help her out.

"No. Just stay there," the attendant says. "We're getting help."

Now there are a bunch of Disney people around, closing off the ride at the entrance, helping people out who were stuck in the middle, talking on their walkie-talkies. Two women are sitting with Christy, asking her questions and reassuring her.

"Where is the pain? How far along are you? Just stay calm, everything will be fine. Help is on the way."

It seems like a long time but finally the paramedics arrive. They help her out of the Small World boat and I see that there's a watery puddle where Christy was sitting. Suddenly I feel weak in the knees and I have to hold on to the iron railing to keep from falling.

The paramedics work quickly, checking blood pressure, asking questions, hooking up some kind of I.V. I'm so woozy myself I'm not exactly sure what's going on.

Two of the Hamilton chaperones come running up behind another Disneyland security person. It's Mrs. Rosenbloom and another English teacher, Miss Bailey.

"Tell me your name, Honey," Miss Bailey says.

"Christina Calderon," Dashan answers for her.

"I think you have the first part of the alphabet," Miss Bailey says to Mrs. Rosenbloom, who starts shuffling through a cardboard file of permission slips. They show the consent for emergency treatment form, signed by Christy's mom, to the paramedics and to a Disneyland official, and the paramedics begin rolling Christy on a stretcher thing toward an ambulance. I run to catch up. Dashan is right behind her, talking to her. We both try to climb in back with her, but the attendant blocks our way and looks toward the teachers.

"You can't leave the park," Miss Bailey says.

"Why not?" Dashan says.

"The only way any student can leave the park is by the bus they came in on, or if their parents come get them."

"But I'm eighteen," I say.

"It doesn't matter," she says. "Those are the rules."

The ambulance moves slowly away, down the fake Main Street, red lights blinking.

"God, I think someone should be there with Christy,"

Dashan says.

I nod my head in agreement, thinking how frightened she must be.

Mrs. Rosenbloom says to Miss Bailey, "I think they're right. It will take her parents at least forty-five minutes to get here. You call the parents and I'll drive these two to the hospital."

"But . . ."

"That's why I drove down here, so we'd have a car available in case of emergency. I think this situation qualifies."

The attendant tells Mrs. Rosenbloom how to get to the hospital, and Dashan and I follow her out to the parking lot. We park in the Emergency section and go inside. Mrs. Rosenbloom identifies herself and asks about Christy. They say she is being seen by an obstetrician, and show us to a cold, gray waiting room. Mrs. Rosenbloom goes to find a telephone so she can call our parents. I don't know what the big deal is, Dashan and I both are eighteen—adults. Why are we still treated like kids? But she says we're still the school's responsibility on official field trips.

While Mrs. Rosenbloom is off making phone calls, a man comes in and asks if Christy's parents have arrived yet.

"They'll probably be here pretty soon," I say.

He says he's the emergency admitting doctor, or something I don't quite get, and asks, "Which one of you boys is the boyfriend?"

Neither of us speaks.

"Well?"

"I guess I am," Dashan says.

"You guess?"

"I used to be," I say.

"Meaning you're the father of this baby?"

"Yes." I say.

"Well, your baby is trying to get here early and your girlfriend, or whatever, isn't in great shape."

"Will she be okay?" I ask.

"Hard to say yet. The ob/gyn will be able to tell you more later," he says. "Pregnancies with girls this age are sometimes a bit risky."

He turns and leaves as quickly as he appeared. He seems angry. I don't like him. Dashan and I are alone in the room with only the sound of the air conditioning unit humming in the background.

"What do you think the doctor meant, about risky pregnancies?" Dashan asks. "Do you think Christy's going to be okay?"

"I don't know. I hope so."

Dashan says, "I hope the baby's okay. I don't think Christy could handle it if he wasn't."

"He?" I say.

"Yeah, he. The little baby."

"It's a boy?"

"Yeah. Didn't you know that? I guess it's not for sure a boy. The doctor says from the looks of the sonogram, it's almost for certain though."

A boy. A son. All my life, when I've thought about what kind of dad I'd be, and told myself how I'd be a better dad than the one I got, I've pictured myself grown up, like in one of those insurance ads you see in *Time* magazine. I'd be married, living in a big house, probably about thirty. Maybe I thought I'd be like my Uncle Steve. But here I am, with a son on the way, and I don't feel grown up at all. Not even close.

Mrs. Rosenbloom comes back to the waiting room.

"I talked with both your mothers," she says. "They said the same thing you did, you're adults. They'd like you to call back in a few hours, though, when you know more what's happening . . . Have you had any news about Christy's condition?"

We tell her what the doctor told us.

"Well, I hope things turn out all right. It makes no sense to me, this having babies so young."

She sits with us for a while, then says, "I'm going to walk

out front to wait for Christy's parents. Then I'll go back to the park. Congratulations on your scholarships," she says to us both, like she can't think of anything else to say.

After Mrs. Rosenbloom leaves, Dashan says, "I probably should leave before Christy's parents get here. Her dad really doesn't like me."

"Her dad doesn't like any guy who likes Christy."

"Especially not any black guy," Dashan says. "I mean, he gets all crazy if I even call her on the phone. I can see why he doesn't like you, but *I've* never done anything to hurt her."

I want to explain—it's not my fault, she said she was on the pill, etc., etc., but it all sounds worn out to me now. I'm worn out. I rest my arms on the back of the cold, plastic chair and try to make a pillow for my head. I can't get comfortable.

I'm pulled out of sleep by familiar voices. Christy's parents are standing just a few feet away from me, talking to a woman in green hospital clothes—a nurse, I guess. At first I think it's a dream that we're all together in a little square room with plastic furniture and no windows. But slowly my memory comes back—Disneyland, Christy's scream, the watery mess. I look at my watch. Five-thirty A.M.

They're saying something about balancing danger to the mom and danger to the fetus. Dashan and I both stand and walk closer, so we can hear what's being said. We all stand together in a circle, listening to the woman who I thought was a nurse but is really a doctor. Dashan and Mr. Calderon are standing so close their shoulders are touching. I guess we're all so worried everybody forgets to be angry.

The doctor explains that the water bag has ruptured, and that leaves the baby very vulnerable to infection. Also, Christy's blood pressure is higher than it should be, which can be dangerous to her if it can't be brought down.

Christy's dad asks, "Is my daughter's life in danger?" at the same time that Dashan asks, "Will she lose the baby?"

"It is highly unlikely that either of those things will happen," the doctor says. "But the situation is serious and she needs to be very closely monitored. We'll admit her to the antepartum unit, try to bring down her blood pressure and hold off on labor. We can also better protect her against infection by keeping her in that unit. She is apparently in her thirty-first week. There's a much better chance of getting a healthy baby if we can keep it in the womb for another couple of weeks. Luckily this hospital has an excellent antepartum and neonatal unit. Christy is better off here than she would be in most other hospitals."

My head is spinning. I only understand half what the doctor is saying, but I understand enough to know that things aren't looking great right now.

"You can go see your daughter for a few minutes now, if you'd like," the doctor says. "But we don't want any excitement or emotional stress, so be sure to stay calm and to reassure her. We don't want her worried or upset. Can you do that?"

"Yes," Mrs. Calderon says.

All of us, including Christy's mom, are looking straight at her dad. If anybody's going to pass around the old emotional stress, he's the one to do it. But he says, "I just want my daughter and my grandson to be healthy. I can be strong for that."

"Which one of you is Dashan?" the doctor asks.

Dashan lifts his hand.

"Christina's been asking for you, so as soon as her parents come out, you can go in. But only for a few minutes."

16

Dress shirt, tie, dark socks, black dress pants, jeans, sweatshirt, what am I missing? Oh yeah, underwear. I check the zippered pocket of my backpack one more time. There it is, a round trip ticket on American Airlines LAX to New Orleans. God. I can hardly believe it. Three hours from now Jeremy, Trin, Mr. Rogers and I are going to be flying high out of L.A.

I look at the trophies lining the top of my bookshelf. When I first started debate, in the ninth grade, I didn't think I'd ever take first place in anything. Now, I have a secret hope that maybe I could get a national trophy. I doubt it, because the competition at nationals is unbelievable. Mr. Rogers says both Jeremy and I have a chance. But really, I've already got my scholarship.

I'm happy just to be competing in New Orleans. Jeremy and I are going to take in the jazz clubs and Bourbon Street. I finally started listening to the tapes Jeremy kept forcing on me, so I'm starting to get into jazz a little bit.

It helped that I saw the TV special about Preservation Hall, which is a place where a lot of jazz musicians, beginners and old-timers both, play. I never would have watched it if I weren't going to New Orleans, but it was very interesting. I can picture myself there, listening to a jazz saxophonist, someone like John Coltrane maybe. It's packed in there, hot, but I don't care. The music surrounds me. I am lost in my fantasy when an insistent note overcomes my imagined saxophone riff. The phone.

"Hello."

"Jeffrey?"

"Yes," I say, recognizing Mrs. Calderon's voice.

"Christy's blood pressure is too high. They've scheduled a cesarean for two-thirty this afternoon." There is a long pause, and then, between sobs, she says, "I thought you should know."

"But they were supposed to hold off for at least another week!"

"Yes, but the blood pressure. It is too risky."

"But will the baby be okay? This early?"

"I pray for them both, *mi hijo*," she says, and then the phone goes dead.

A cesarean at two-thirty. My plane leaves at eleven. Mom knocks on my bedroom door and opens it a crack. She's still in her nurse's uniform, just home from the night shift at Hamilton Hospital. She smiles when she sees my suitcase all packed and ready to go.

"You're going to have a wonderful time, Jeff. I'm so excited for you—and proud . . . Who was on the phone?"

"Christy's mom," I say.

"Oh? Anything wrong?"

I tell her about the scheduled surgery.

"It's pretty routine," my mom says. "It can be serious, but usually these things turn out okay."

"I don't know what to do," I say. "I've wanted this for so long . . ."

"I know. You've had your heart set on going to a national competition. And in such a wonderful, exciting city . . ."

"Yeah. And I don't want to let Mr. Rogers down, either, or the rest of the team."

"Or Jeremy . . ."

"Yeah. But I don't know. I mean, it's not like I can do anything here. Christy doesn't even want to see me. I'd just be in the way . . ."

Mom doesn't say anything more—just stands there looking at me. Then she comes over to where I'm sitting on the bed, puts her arms around me and hugs me long and hard. "I wish things were different for you. And poor Christy—I still wish she'd consider adoption. That's a strange thing for a grandmother to say, but I feel so sorry for this little guy coming into the world where no one is really prepared to take care of him. I always thought how much fun I'd have as a grandmother, how much I would love your children, but I wasn't expecting it to be like this."

I don't want to look at my mom. I'm afraid I'll see tears in her eyes. For about the millionth time I wonder how I let my life get so messed up, and for about the billionth time I'm pissed at Christy. But what can I do? What can anyone do now?

Mom sighs and shakes her head sadly. As if she'd read my mind she says, "I wish I had an easy answer for you, Jeffie, but there's no such thing at this stage of the game." We sit next to each other on the edge of the bed, not talking. Finally she says, "I'm going to hop in the shower. Let me know what you decide to do."

I go over and over stuff in my head. I can't be of any help to Christy or the baby. I've got my ticket, my hotel room, my dreams. Damn it! I've got my dreams!

I sit for a long time, trying to convince myself that going to New Orleans is the right thing to do. But a refrain starts in my head that is stronger than any free-floating melody I would hear at Preservation Hall. My son will be born today. My son will be born today. Over and over again, drowning out the story I'm telling myself about how I will go on to New Orleans. My son will be born today.

Why can't I find anything? I know I've got Mr. Rogers' phone number around here somewhere. It's on one of those little yellow Post-it things. I look under my books, in my jacket pocket. Where is it? Shit! I throw the clothes from my suitcase on the floor and grab one item at a time, checking all the pockets and throwing it back again.

Mom comes into my room, wrapped in her oversized terry-cloth robe, towel-drying her hair. She stops and looks down at the pile of clothes in the middle of my room.

"Aren't you going?" she asks.

"Does it look like I'm going?" I shout, rummaging through the pockets of my jeans.

"Hey, Jeff. Remember me? I'm with you."

I throw the jeans back on the floor and empty my backpack out onto the bed.

"Looking for something?" Mom asks.

"Yeah. I can't find Mr. Rogers' phone number."

She walks over to my desk and picks up a piece of paper from next to my phone.

"Is this it?"

"I hate this shit!" I say.

"What shit?" she asks, neatly stacking the books and papers I've just dumped from my backpack and sitting on the edge of my bed.

"All of this shit! How you can always find stuff and I can't! How I'm going to miss the debate tournament. I hate letting everybody down. What if Christy dies? What if the baby doesn't come out right—like what if he doesn't have a brain, or a heart or something?"

Mom stands and puts her arms around me. "Remember when Steve was going to that support group, I think it was called a grief group, after Janie died?"

"I remember."

"And remember the famous prayer he had taped to his bathroom mirror?"

"Sort of."

"God grant me the serenity to accept that which I cannot change, the courage to change that which I can, and the wisdom to know the difference."

"I don't even think there *is* a god," I say.

"It doesn't matter. Think of the prayer as good advice."
Mom moves away from me, toward the door.

"I'm going to take a short rest now. I'm pooped. But wake
me after you've made your phone calls and before you go
wherever it is you end up going this morning."

First I call Mr. Rogers. When I tell him I can't go to New
Orleans because the baby is going to be born today, there
is a long silence. Then he says, "I'd heard you weren't going
to have anything to do with this baby— it was all Christy's
fault, so it was only her baby."

"I can't help it," I say. "I can't explain how I feel. I just
know I have to be at the hospital when the baby is born."

There is another long silence, then, "Of course babies
are more important than debate tournaments. But I'm
disappointed that you won't be there, Jeff. This will make
a big difference in how Hamilton places."

"I know," I say. "I'm sorry."

"Well, follow your conscience. I hope everything goes
fine for Christy and the baby. I'll talk to you when we get
back."

He hangs up without saying goodbye. I sit holding the
phone, staring at the clothes still in a heap in the middle
of the floor. It would have been easier if Rogers had yelled
at me—told me what a fool I was for messing things up.

I punch in Jeremy's number. He answers. I tell him I'm
going to the hospital instead of New Orleans.

"You can't do that," he says. "That screws up the whole
tournament for Hamilton High."

"I've already been through that with Mr. Rogers," I say.

Jeremy tells me the same stuff I started out telling
myself, that there's nothing I can do to help at the hospital,
that New Orleans is a once-in-a-lifetime chance, that I
probably can't get a refund on my ticket, everything I've
already thought about.

Finally, we wish each other luck and I hang up.

I pick my clothes up off the floor and stuff my suitcase into the back of my closet. I go into the den and flop down on the couch in front of the TV. I punch the remote, unthinkingly spinning past "Family Feud" and "I Love Lucy," "Sesame Street" and something with Daffy Duck quacking his head off.

After about ten boring runs through the channels, I pause at "Oprah." I stop there because she's interviewing some guys who look to be about my age. It turns out that they're all teen dads involved in custody battles. I shut off the TV and sit staring at the blank screen. There's a lot I don't want to think about.

By noon I decide I might as well head on down to the hospital. Jeremy and the rest of the debaters are probably somewhere over Arizona by now, and I'm headed for the same old freeway in the same old L.A. Basin. Maybe they're over the Grand Canyon and Jeremy is trying to convince the pilot to fly low.

It isn't until I've backed halfway down the driveway that I remember Mom asked me to wake her before I leave. I turn off the ignition, go back into the house and tiptoe into her bedroom. She is lying on her bed, staring at the ceiling. One of her big nursing books is open beside her.

"I'm leaving now. I'm going to the hospital."

"Let me throw some clothes on. I'll go, too."

"You don't need to do that, Mom. You're tired."

"But I'm a nurse. I know the right questions to ask. Besides, I guess I'm about to become a grandmother."

I wait in the car while mom gets dressed. She comes out carrying a brush and a make-up bag.

"By the time we get there I'll be presentable," she says.

We drive in silence, the San Bernardino Freeway to the 605, then south toward Anaheim. My mom never looks like she wears much make-up. Not like Barb, down at Barb and Edie's, who looks like she applies the stuff with a spatula. But I guess Mom wears more than I think, because each time I glance at her she's adding something to her face—

lipstick, blush, eye stuff. She's using the mirror that
Christy bought and attached to the back of the visor on the
passenger side, a long, long time ago, after we'd first started kissing off her lipstick and getting her hair messed up.

"I reviewed the ob/gyn section of my nursing book this
morning," Mom says, folding back the visor and putting
her make-up in her purse.

"What section?"

"Obstetrical, you know, having to do with pregnancy
and birth. Apparently high blood pressure is a very common thing with young mothers. And girls seventeen and
younger are at higher risk for premature labor. How far
along is Christy?"

"The doctor said thirty-one on Grad Nite."

"So . . . almost thirty-three weeks," Mom says, as much
to herself as to me. "They really like to hold things off until
at least thirty-four weeks."

"So why are they doing surgery then?" I ask.

"High blood pressure can be very dangerous to Christy.
Her system may be poisoning her, so they have to risk
taking the baby this early."

"But only about a week earlier than they first said. A
week won't make much difference, will it?"

"Every day counts at this stage. Brain cells are still
being formed, the lungs are still developing. A lot happens
during the last six weeks of a normal pregnancy."

Is she saying he won't have a brain that works right if
he's born today? I'm afraid to ask. We're quiet for about ten
miles, then Mom says, "I remember the day you were born.
I thought you were the most beautiful baby in the world. So
did your dad. He was nuts about you when you were born."

"Then what happened?" I asked. "Didn't he like the way
I was turning out by the time I was five?"

"No, I don't think that. I think he still loves you in his
own limited way. He's so immature, he doesn't know how
to care deeply for someone else."

"*I'm* immature. I'm too young to be a dad."

"So . . . how about working on the serenity to accept that which you cannot change?"

How about butting out, I think but don't say. I know none of this is my mom's fault, but everything annoys me right now. I'm in a really bad mood, but I'm afraid it's not my mood. It's my life.

I turn the news station on and hear that we're breathing the stuff that makes for third stage smog alerts. Also, there's been a fatal accident on the San Diego Freeway, south of Laguna Beach. I turn the radio off. Just past the place where my grandma always says how there used to be nothing but orange groves here, I get off the freeway.

At the hospital Mom and I find the waiting room where Dashan and I hung out when we first brought Christy here on Grad Nite. Mr. Calderon is sitting in there flipping the pages of an old *Life* magazine. I was hoping to see Mrs. Calderon instead, but why should I expect to be lucky? He looks up at us as we walk into the room.

"They were able to take Christy to surgery early," he says. "She went in about one. Olga is in the chapel."

"What do the doctors say?" Mom asks.

"I don't know. Doctors. Who can understand what they're saying? 'Don't worry,' they're saying, but it's not their daughter.

"They told us one of us could be in there, for the birth, but I knew I couldn't stand to see them cut into my daughter, and neither could Olga."

It's strange, I think, how worried he is about a knife cut, under anesthetic, when he seems to enjoy hurting people so much with his words. I'll never understand this guy.

"I think I'll go see what I can find out," Mom says. "Do you mind?"

Mr. Calderon shakes his head. My mom walks out, leaving the two of us alone. As much as I don't like Christy's dad, I see the worry and sadness in his face and my attitude toward him softens. He goes back to *Life* magazine and I pick up a dog-eared copy of *People*.

When my mom comes back Mrs. Calderon is with her.

"I talked with one of the nurses," Mom says. "Christy should be out of surgery in another thirty minutes or so."

Mrs. Calderon sinks into the chair next to Christy's dad. They hold hands, not looking at one another.

It seems forever before the doctor comes into the waiting room. We all stand. I don't know why, we just do.

"Everything looks good," she says. "They'll be moving Christy to her room in a few minutes. Her vital signs have stabilized and her blood pressure is approaching a normal range. The baby, a boy, as you already knew, weighs three pounds fifteen ounces. He's already in the N.I.C.U.

"Where?" I ask.

"N.I.C.U.," Mom says. "Neonatal Intensive Care Unit. That's where all premature babies go at first, so they can be closely monitored."

"Right," the doctor says. "You're welcome to go take a look at him. Just follow the signs and buzz the nurse when you get to the double doors."

Mrs. Calderon is crying, saying over and over, "Is she all right? Is he all right? Doctor?"

"As I said, everything looks good. She's stabilized. As for the baby, with preemies the first twenty-four hours tells a lot, but he's been checked out by the neonatologist and he doesn't seem to have any major problems. . . Come on, I'll take you to see your daughter," the doctor says, taking Mrs. Calderon by the arm. Mr. Calderon follows along.

"I'm going to see the baby," I say.

"It's this way," Mom says, slipping her arm around my shoulder and steering me in the direction of the N.I.C.U. place. "You know, Jeff, he won't look like one of those Gerber babies."

"What do you mean?"

"I mean, preemies are so small and fragile looking they aren't exactly cute.

17

A nurse meets us at the double doors. "Which baby would you like to see?" she asks. "Who's the mother?"

"Christina Calderon," Mom answers.

"Are you family?"

"Father and grandmother," Mom says.

The nurse motions us through the door and points to a large sink. "You'll have to scrub up and wear a sterile gown," she says. "It's very important to keep a sterile environment for these babies. Take off any rings, watches or bracelets and put them in your pockets or purse. If you're carrying a purse you can leave it over there at the desk before you scrub."

My mom takes off her rings and watch, puts them in her jeans pocket, steps up to the sink and begins washing.

"Use plenty of soap," the nurse says. "Backs and fronts of hands, wrists and forearms up to elbows, between fingers . . ."

She isn't even looking as she talks. She probably says the same thing about forty times a day. It's like a recording.

Mom finishes scrubbing and dons a sterile gown. Smiling, she says to the nurse. "I'm a nurse, too, so I know the routine."

It's as if my mom has said the magic word. The nurse, who has so far been like a robot, suddenly turns human. While I scrub and put on a gown she chats away.

"Your first grandchild?"

"Yes."

"You're a very young grandmother."

"Younger than I expected to be when I got that title."

The nurse laughs. "Our kids surprise us sometimes, don't they? Have you ever worked N.I.C.U.?"

"No. Except for a brief stint during training. Actually, I must confess I've only been a nurse for a few weeks."

"Well, but you know what to expect with the babies, don't you?"

Mom nods. God. I hope they're not a bunch of freaks or something. The way they talk, I'm afraid to go in there. Maybe I should wait outside and just have my mom go in. What can I do? She's the nurse. But all the time I'm thinking this, mom is gripping the sleeve of my hospital gown, pulling me along to where the babies are kept.

"I don't know if I want to see him or not," I say.

"You've come this far. I'll go in with you."

The nurse, who now is acting like she and my mom are best friends, leads us into a room where there are about fifteen plastic containers, not much bigger than milk crates, all with babies in them.

"Calderon?" she says to another nurse who is checking a chart.

This nurse looks up and smiles. "Yes—just in. He's in the middle incubator over there," she says, pointing.

My mom's new best friend walks over and checks a card on the container—incubator, I guess they call it.

"Here he is, Daddy," she says, then stands back so we can get a good look. God! He's tiny! How can a person that little stay alive? He's all scrawny and wrinkly. He's lying on his back, with only a diaper on. His long skinny legs are drawn up, and he's got tubes attached to him everywhere. God! What's wrong with him? My heart is racing. I look over at my mom. She looks calm.

"What's wrong with him?" I ask in a whisper.

"I don't know that anything's wrong with him, except he got here too soon."

"But *look* at him! And look at all that stuff he's hooked up to."

"He weighs less than four pounds, Jeff. His body isn't quite ready for the world. The tubes in his nostrils deliver oxygen. His lungs aren't fully developed yet. The teddy-bear shaped band-aid thing on his chest secures a sensor that sets off the breathing monitor alarm if he stops breathing."

"What do you mean, stops breathing?"

"It's very common for preemies to forget to breathe now and then. When the monitor goes off a nurse runs over and pats the baby, or rubs the soles of its feet. Usually that's all it takes."

I follow the line from the baby to a machine that's got constantly changing numbers on a screen that's big enough to see from across the room.

"What about that thing in his mouth?"

"A feeding tube. It's probably too hard for him to suck yet. And they want to be sure he's getting the right amount of food."

My mom sticks her hand through one of the big holes on the side of the incubator and rubs her finger along his leg.

"Should you touch him?"

"Sure. Preemies need to be touched, just like any other baby."

"What's all that other stuff attached to him?"

"Let's see. He's got a heart monitor. The tube attached to his belly button is for blood tests, so they don't need to poke him each time. That's it. Breathing, feeding, heart and blood."

We stand together, me and my mom, looking down at the scrawny little baby. I reach my hand through the other opening and run my finger along his arm. After a while my mom tells me she's going to find Christy's mom and talk to her about the baby, so she'll be prepared to see him all hooked up.

I stay, watching the baby. His whole arm is not much longer than my longest finger, and not much bigger around than my thumb. He is an amazing and frightening sight. I run my finger gently along the inside of his arm to the palm of his hand. He closes his fist around my finger. I can't believe it! He's got a grip!

I see those tiny fingers holding on to my one, comparatively huge, index finger. I watch his chest rise and fall with each breath, matching his irregular breathing with my own, as if I'm willing him to breathe. Gently, I straighten his little closed fist. There it is—his pinky finger— crooked as a dog's hind leg.

Something wells up inside me. All of these months of trying to avoid the thought of this baby, of my son, are as far behind me as the Dark Ages. My son. I remember the words I've heard so often when Dashan gives his Dramatic Interpretation at debate tournaments. The spirit of Kunta Kinte crosses boundaries of time and culture, reminding me of what is important for fathers to pass on to sons. "He was going to teach this manchild to be a true man, no matter what trials and hazards that might involve . . . For it was the job of a father to be as a giant tree to his manchild."

I lean my head against the hard plastic incubator. "Okay. You've got me," I whisper to the skin and bones, crooked fingered, pre-person. "Even though I'm not yet a true man myself, I'm trying to be one, and I'll help you be one too."

I touch the bottom of his foot, wishing he'd open his eyes, but he doesn't. He just lies there, breathing, his chest moving up and down, up and down, while everything about him is being recorded on machines that look like something from Star Trek. There is a plastic band attached to his ankle that says C. Calderon on it. I notice a blue three by five card attached to the side of the incubator. It says:

> *CALDERON*
> *Delivering doctor: Somonion*
> *Birth date: June 24, 1:30 p.m.*
> *Mother: Christina Teresa Calderon*
> *Wt: 1770 grams   Ht: 42 cm.*
> *Pediatrician: Nahvi*

I wish I could remember the grams and centimeter stuff from math, but I can't. I'm pretty sure the nurse said he weighed three pounds fifteen ounces. I don't know how long he is. I pull my hand out of the incubator and hold my arm lengthwise along the side. He is not quite as long as from my elbow to my knuckles.

The nurse who let us in comes and stands beside me.

"He's a beautiful little baby," she says.

I wonder if she's had her eyes checked lately, but say nothing.

"The grandparents want to see this little guy now, Daddy. We don't like to have too many people in here at one time. Maybe you could go down to the coffee shop and come back later?"

She says it like a question, but I know it's an order. I see Mr. and Mrs. Calderon standing at the sink, being told how to wash. I stop.

"Is Christy okay?" I ask.

"The doctor says she is," Mrs. Calderon says. She looks very tired, and sad. Mr. Calderon doesn't look at me.

I find my mom in the coffee shop. The minute I walk through the door I realize how hungry I am. I sit down and order a cheeseburger and fries. Mom has the remains of a salad on her plate.

"Did you see Christy?" I ask.

"Yes, for a few minutes."

"Her mom looked really worried when I saw her just now."

"Well, no one looks great right after surgery. Christy

looks pale, and she's hooked up to various monitors, too. She may be a bit depressed, but that's not unusual. I don't think there's anything to worry about."

The cheeseburger tastes like sawdust. I add about a ton of catsup, so now it tastes like sawdust with catsup. Oh, well. Maybe I'm not as hungry as I thought.

"Are you going home soon, or should I call Steve and see if he can come get me?" Mom asks. "I'm scheduled to be at work at midnight, and I need a few hours sleep in between."

"What time is it?"

"Six-thirty. I'd take the night off, but one nurse is out sick and another's on vacation. I should go in if I possibly can."

"I'll take you home," I say. "But maybe I'll see Christy first. Should I?"

"I think that's a good idea. Seeing you might cheer her up."

"Or it might make her feel worse. What do you think?"

"I think you're parents now, and you've got to figure out how to get along."

"Like you and dad?" I say.

We both laugh. It's the first laugh I've had all day, and it feels good.

"But Jeff, your father and I do manage to speak, and to be civil to each other, especially in matters concerning you. It's not ideal, but life seldom is."

"I can see that," I say.

I give Mom the keys to my car so she can wait for me there, and she tells me how to find Christy. There are three other girls, women, whatever, in the room with Christy. It's another one of those intensive care, Star Wars kind of places. I pull a chair up next to Christy's bed. She is very pale. I wonder how it is that a person with dark skin can look so light.

"Christy?"

She opens her eyes and looks at me. I can see she's been

crying.

"How are you doing?"

"Okay," she sighs.

"I saw the baby," I tell her.

Her eyes fill with tears. "He's ugly. He looks like a rat," she says, breaking into full-fledged sobbing.

I think of his little chest, rising and falling with each laborious breath. "He's working hard to live," I say. She doesn't answer, just keeps crying. "But I thought this was what you wanted."

"I thought so, too, but I made a mistake," she says, turning her face away from me. "I didn't know he would look like a rat."

A nurse comes in to check her blood pressure and I leave, feeling helpless. I'm walking to the car when I remember what Mrs. Gould told me about getting my name on the birth certificate. The baby's band and the card on his incubator only have Christy's name on them. Christina Calderon, who can't say anything about him except he looks like a rat. I don't even exist as far as any hospital records are concerned. I run back to the neonatal unit and find the nurse my mom and I had talked with earlier.

"I want to be sure my name is on the birth certificate," I say.

The nurse picks up a phone and punches in some numbers.

"I have a father down here who wants to know if his name got on the baby's birth certificate—Calderon, Christina, is the mother's name." There is a long pause, then she hangs up.

"Medical records says they're waiting until tomorrow morning to fill out the birth certificate. They like to get the baby's name on it, and apparently Christina isn't ready to name the baby."

A name. I haven't even thought about a name.

"Can't I at least get *my* name on it now?"

"No. It's not ready. Christina is rather upset. Morning

will be a better time. The birth clerk will probably be taking a birth certificate information form to Christina's room around ten in the morning. You can come back then."

I go out to the car. My mom is curled up in the passenger seat, sound asleep. I get in and start the engine but she doesn't stir.

"Mom?" I poke her gently on the arm. "Mom?"

"Uh," she says, not moving.

"Buckle up."

She fumbles around with the seat belt, not opening her eyes, and finally gets it fastened. I drive the forty-five minutes home, lost in thought. I am surprised to find myself turning into our driveway. I have no memory of getting from the hospital to our house.

Mom stumbles through the door and into her bedroom, then calls to me. I walk down the hall.

"What?"

"You should probably phone some people and tell them about the baby."

"Like who?"

"Like Steve, and your grandma, and your father too, I guess."

I look at my mom, flopped across her bed, still in her clothes, big bags under her eyes. I know I've caused her plenty of worry and disappointment these past few months. And, except for rare moments of shock or anger, she's accepted me for who I am. I walk over and sit on the edge of her bed.

"Thanks, Mom, for going with me today. It really helped to have you there."

"You're welcome, Jeffie. I love you," she says, taking my hand and kissing it.

"I love you, too, Mom," I say, kissing her forehead.

I go back to the kitchen to make phone calls. It's strange. Everyone in my family, including me, thought Christy's pregnancy was a major disaster. But now, when I call Steve, then my grandma, and tell them about the baby, it's like they already love him. In spite of Christy's talk, there's a lot of love going out to my little son.

After I call Steve and Grandma I dial my dad's number. I really don't feel like talking to old HANK 40 tonight, but I may as well get it over with.

"Let me get this straight. Your ex-girlfriend just had a baby?" he says.

"Right. A boy."

"That's about the most stupid thing you've ever done," he says. "Don't sign anything. She can't prove anything. Take my word for it, you don't want to be paying support on this kid for the next eighteen years."

"Thanks for the advice," I say, and hang up.

I go to my room, put a Duke Ellington CD on the stereo, put on my headphones and crank it up. I lie stretched out on my bed, looking at the airline ticket envelope still sitting on top of my dresser. It seems like about five years have passed since early this morning, when I thought I was on my way to New Orleans.

18

It's six in the morning and I'm wide awake, wondering how the baby is doing. And Christy. God, what's with her, anyway? I'll go to the hospital in time to check out the birth certificate stuff. Steve wants to go with me and I'll be glad for company. In the meantime, though, I can't just lie in bed with my brain buzzing.

I put on sweats and running shoes and drive to the Fitness Club. The first person I see is Faye, pumping iron at ten pounds a weight.

"Hey, Faye," I greet her on my way to the Stairmaster.

She stops, mid-lift. "Hey yourself, Browning. I thought you were in New Orleans wowing people with your highly polished dramatic skills."

"Something came up," I say.

"Tell your old Granny Faye," she says, patting the bench beside her.

"Well . . . It's kind of a long story. Come see me on the Stairmaster before you leave," I say. "I want to grab one before they're all taken."

Joe notices me from across the room. "I thought we weren't going to see you for a while."

"It's a long story," Faye says.

"I'm sure you'll know every detail before you leave today," Joe says to Faye, laughing. "Are you keeping the same work schedule we've got you signed up for next weekend, Jeff?"

"Yes. Except if you need someone before then, I can fill in."

I climb onto the Stairmaster and start my routine. A name, I think. What will Christy want to name the baby? What would be a good name? Something short and modern—not nerdy like Elmer or Horace. Maybe Damian, or Shawn. What goes good with Browning? I don't want him to be named after anyone because I want him to be his own person.

My shirt is wet, sticking to my back, and sweat is rolling down my face when Faye scoots into the space between the machines. She still walks with a limp, but she no longer needs a cane—pretty amazing. She taps me on the arm and says, "Talk!"

"I just had a baby last night," I tell her.

"And already exercising this morning! Talk about the miracles of modern science," she says, cackling.

"He was premature—not quite four pounds," I say.

Her smile fades. "Is he all right?"

I tell her all I know. Then she says, "Why didn't I know you were going to be a father? I thought we were sweethearts—or were you just leading me on?"

"I didn't want to talk about it, or think about it. It wasn't my idea."

"And the mother? Is she the one who used to be hanging around all the time when I first started coming here? She made me so jealous, that cute little Mexicali Rose did."

"Christina," I say. Old people can be really racist sometimes without even knowing it.

"One thing I know about you, Jeff, is you'll do the right thing," Faye says.

"I'm not going to marry her, if that's what you mean."

She cackles again. "Of course that's not what I mean. I'm

a modern girl, don't you know? I'm quite aware that getting married just because you got someone pregnant went out during the Proterozoic era . . . I only mean I can't see you running away from your paternal responsibilities."

"I know," I say. "I guess I can't see me doing that either."

Steve and I go directly to the N.I.C.U. section. We scrub and put on hospital gowns and a nurse buzzes us through the doors. I'm shocked to see that in addition to all the other stuff they've got on the baby, he's now wearing some kind of blinder things.

"What's this?" I ask one of the nurses.

She walks over to where we're standing. "The eye patches?"

"Yeah. What's wrong with his eyes?" I think how I haven't even seen his eyes yet. Maybe he doesn't have any eyes.

"He has to be under special lights for a while. The eye patches are simply for protection."

I see now that there is a bright light shining down on him.

"Why does he need the lights?" Steve asks.

"He's becoming a bit jaundiced. See how his skin has a yellowish tinge? It's very common in newborns, and especially in preemies. It takes a while for their liver to start doing all it needs to do. It's usually not serious."

The nurse turns the light out, reaches in through the opening and takes the blinders off. "The lights don't have to be on him constantly. You can reach through the portholes and touch him, introduce yourselves, talk to him. These tiny ones need plenty of touching and talking to, just like the bigger ones do . . . What's his name?" she asks, checking the blue card.

"I don't know yet," I say.

"He needs a name soon," the nurse says. "You'd be surprised how quickly these babies learn to respond to their names."

A few minutes before ten I leave Steve talking to the baby, telling him what a wonderful great-uncle he has, and I go upstairs to Christy's room. The woman from medical records is already there, writing information on a form attached to a clipboard. Christy's mom and dad are there, too. "Hi," I say.

They all look up, but only the woman with the clipboard, the birth certificate clerk, says hello. Then she turns her attention back to Christy and starts reading from the form.

"Mother: Christina Teresa Calderon. Right?"

Christy nods.

"Date and time of birth, doctor's name . . ." She reads off a list of things, then asks "Father's name?"

I wait for Christy to answer, but she doesn't. "Jeffrey Dean Browning," I say.

"Is that correct?" the clerk asks.

No one answers.

"You can always put 'unknown' in this space if you're not sure who the father is," the clerk says.

"I'm the father," I say. "Jeffrey Dean Browning. That's the name that goes in that space!"

"Christina?" the clerk asks.

Christy doesn't answer. Finally, after what seems like a long time, Mr. Calderon says, "Yes, Christina. You must put Jeff's name on the certificate. The baby must have a father. It's important for his baptism."

Christy nods to the clerk, who then asks for the correct spelling of my name and writes it on the form.

"Name of baby?" the clerk asks.

Again, no one speaks. I can see that the clerk is getting annoyed.

"Christina, it is important for us to file your baby's birth certificate, if for no other reason than that he can then begin to get Medi-Cal. The neonatal unit is extremely costly. And the baby needs a name anyway, so you can start thinking of him as a person and not just as the baby."

"How about naming him Alfredo, after your father?" Mrs. Calderon asks.

"I don't care," Christy says.

God, my son is going to be named after one of the men I dislike most in the world. Not only that, I'll be reminded of fettucini whenever I hear his name.

"How about Andrew?" I say. I don't care all that much for the name Andrew either, but it's the first thing that comes to my mind and it's a thousand times better than Alfredo.

The clerk looks from me to Christy and back again.

"I'll tell you what," she says, taking a small paperback book from her pocket and handing it to Christy. "Let's leave the mother and father alone for a few minutes. Have you grandparents seen your grandson yet this morning?"

Mr. and Mrs. Calderon both shake their heads no.

"Well, maybe now is a good time. And Christina and Jeffrey here can look through this little book of names and make a decision."

So the Calderons leave, and so does the clerk, and Christy just lies there, flat on her back, staring out the window.

I take the book from her and begin reading names.

"Alexander—helper of men? Or Curtis—courteous? Or Eric—uncertain meaning? How about Ethelred—noble counsel?" I say, hoping for a laugh, a smile, a sign of life.

"I really don't care," she sighs.

"How about Luke? I like how that sounds."

She turns on me, furious. "I said I don't care! Name him whatever the hell you want!"

I feel everyone else in the room looking at us, other new mothers and visitors, and I can feel the back of my neck glowing. Christy turns her face to the window again and I continue reading, silently, from the book of names.

When the clerk comes back I tell her the baby's name will be Ethan Calderon Browning. She looks at Christy, who says nothing, then writes the name on the form and hands it to Christy to sign. Christy doesn't even bother to read the form. She just signs it and looks out the window again.

I don't know why I chose Ethan, except that I like the sound, and it means strength, and I think he's going to need a lot of strength to get through his life—even to get started. And it sure beats Alfredo. I gave Calderon for a middle name because I think his mother's family name should be in there somewhere, but Browning should definitely be his last name.

It's not until hours later that I think of Ethan Canin, the guy who wrote the story I would be using for Dramatic Interpretation in New Orleans this very day, if I'd made it to New Orleans. And I thought I didn't want my son named after anyone. Oh well, it has a nice ring to it, anyway.

On the way home I tell Steve about how Christy acted.

"I was leaving the nursery just as her mom and dad were coming in," he says. "I heard a nurse talking to them, telling them that new mothers, especially mothers of preemies, are likely to be depressed for a few days, maybe even weeks, after they give birth."

"She acts like she doesn't even want the baby now that she's had him."

Steve is quiet for a long time, then says, "Maybe now is the time to bring up the possibility of adoption again."

"I don't know," I say. "It seemed like a great idea a few months ago, but now . . ."

"Well, no hurry. You and Christy could decide on that months from now if you want. Of course, the sooner the easier for everyone, I suppose."

I look over at Steve, trying to read him, but I can't tell if he thinks it's a good idea, or a rotten idea. I ask him.

"Just a plain old idea," he says. "You're at a place in life now where I can't possibly think I know what's right for you. I just know that somehow you'll figure it out."

"I hope so," I say.

After dinner I try to call Jeremy at the hotel in New Orleans, but he's out. I leave a message for him to call me, no matter how late it is when he gets in. It is after midnight when the phone rings.

"Hey, J.B. what's the haps?"

I tell him all about the baby, and how Christy couldn't even be bothered to name him.

"She's a nut case," was Jeremy's considered opinion. "How's New Orleans?"

"You're missing out, Daddy-O. It's like one big party on the streets at night—guys standing on the sidewalk, playing the sax or trombone, there's this trio—a keyboard, bass, and woman singing very sultry songs who play all night long. It's after two here now and they were still playing when I walked past them on my way to the hotel."

"How about the tournament?"

"Rogers was all agitated when we got on the plane. He hardly spoke to me, as if it were my fault you were having a baby."

"But how did you do in the competition today?"

"Hold your horses. I'm getting to that . . . As soon as the plane landed, before we even checked into the hotel, Rogers hurried over to the tournament headquarters and checked the national ratings to see who would be next in line. There was the girl from Sacramento who does the D.I. from 'Six Degrees of Separation.' Remember her?"

"Yeah. She always scares me when I have to compete against her. She's really good."

"Well, she was next in line after you, so the big chief organizer called to see if she could compete on such short notice. But her mom said the girl was white water rafting down the American River—no portable phones on the rafts I guess. Then they tried to reach the next guy, but he's in Cancun. So guess who's next?"

"How would I know? Who?"

"Guess."

"One of those girls we hung around with at Disneyland?

One of the 'D' girls?"

"No. Better than that. It's a 'D' name, though."

"Dashan?"

"Yes! Is that not magnificent? Rogers called right away, reached Dashan, *bought* an airplane ticket for him, and Dashan was banging on my door at midnight."

"Rogers paid for Dashan's ticket?"

"Well, Dashan will pay him back. He didn't have the money right now is all. And your room and meal ticket is already paid for, so that's no problem."

I think about how I worked overtime to pay for my hotel and meals. Oh well, they wouldn't have given me a refund. At least someone from Hamilton High gets to use it.

"So Dashan is taking my place in D.I., but what about the Policy Debate? He and Patrick didn't even get into Finals at the qualifier."

"I know. I thought I was absolutely knocked out of Policy Debate when you told me you weren't going. Up shit creek without a paddle. But Rogers made this special appeal. At first it looked like Dashan couldn't be my partner, but then someone found some seldom used rule somewhere and it's going to work. Is that not the cat's meow?"

"But Dashan doesn't know how we work together. Will you have a chance to place without me?"

"I don't know, but I'm happy to have a chance to try. I'm still up shit creek, but at least now I have a paddle."

"How's D.I. going?"

"Dashan made finals."

"How about Trin?"

"She's out of D.I., but still in with Extemporaneous."

"How about Oratory?"

"I'm in, my man."

"Call me tomorrow night—let me know how Finals go."

Here's what happened in New Orleans. Dashan took third place in D.I. and he and Jeremy took third in Policy

Debate. Jeremy said he was pretty sure we'd have won it if I'd been along, but who knows? Jeremy took first in Extemp and Trin took second in Oratory.

It was the first time in twenty-two years that a single school had walked off with five trophies in an NFL national tournament. It must have been exciting to be there . . . plus they did a bayou tour and now Jeremy's in love with Cajun music.

Well, what can I say? I missed the chance of a lifetime, but I got to meet that crooked-fingered little baby when he was only an hour old. I chose right, but *damn*, I wish I could have had both experiences.

19

By the time little Ethan is three weeks old he's gained enough weight that he doesn't look like a bag of bones. He opens his eyes a lot more than he did at first, and he can suck well enough to eat on his own. He doesn't need the oxygen tube anymore. He's still hooked up to a breathing monitor, but so far he hasn't once forgotten to breathe.

Christy was in the hospital for five days because of having a cesarean birth instead of the regular kind. The first three days, the nurses practically forced Christy to go see the baby, and to touch him. Lots of times she'd just sit in the nursery and cry. But she likes Ethan better now that he looks more human.

She still seems kind of down, but the hospital social worker is setting Christy up with group counseling. I guess we both have a lot to work through, now that we're parents. One thing is certain, neither of us considers the possibility of adoption for Ethan. He's ours now, no matter what.

We're bringing him home in two days if everything goes well. Christy's dad painted her room and bought a cradle to put next to her bed. Her mom made new curtains, so everything looks bright and fresh in there. I saw it when I picked Christy up yesterday. Most days we've been going to the hospital together and staying through two feedings. Christy gives him one feeding and I do the next. The nurses taught us how to reach through the portholes to support his head while we feed him, and how to lean him forward to burp him after he eats.

Today Christy and her mother and I are going together to the hospital to take a baby CPR course—not just watch and take notes either. We have to show that we know how to do it before the hospital will let us take the baby home.

Because Christy had the baby in a hospital clear down near Disneyland, it's been more of a big deal to get down there and back every day. Sometimes we've had to carpool. Her mom doesn't drive, and Christy's not supposed to drive yet because of her surgery, and her dad can't get off work, so Christy and her mom often ride with me down to Anaheim. Sometimes my mom goes, too.

I think if Ethan had been born at Hamilton Heights Hospital, where he was supposed to be born, we might still not be talking to each other. But we're learning to get along. Not like we all are best friends, but like we realize we all love the same little person, and that makes it possible for us to talk again.

Christy's dad said hello to me yesterday evening when I brought over some undershirts and nightgowns for when Ethan gets home. One of the tiny nightgowns looks like a baseball uniform. Even Mr. Calderon had to smile when he saw it.

I can't believe I'm buying baby clothes and getting all excited when a baby burps, but that's how things are right now.

I go to the hospital in the morning and see the baby, then work the two to ten shift at the Fitness Club, then start over the next day. When I can, I work extra hours because I'm trying to save money for college *and* buy things for Ethan. Plus all of the gas to and from the hospital costs extra, too.

When we first get to N.I.C.U., Heather, a nurse who often takes care of Ethan, tells us he's graduated. She says the unit where he's been all along is the pre-school and now he's advanced to kindergarten.

She leads us into another room where Ethan is in a little plastic crib, but not an incubator with a top on it. He's wearing an undershirt instead of being shirtless the way I've always seen him, and he's wrapped in a blanket.

Heather explains that they'll keep a close eye on him to be certain he can maintain his body temperature outside the temperature-controlled incubator. It's important to know he can do this before we take him from the hospital.

The three of us all pass the baby CPR requirement, although Mrs. Calderon is very nervous about it. Tomorrow Christy and her mom, who are designated as "primary caregivers," are scheduled to go through "a day with baby." Under Heather's supervision they'll give Ethan a bath, feed him, change him, clean his belly-button, the works. I'm not *required* to be here for this, but I want to, anyway. I think I should be able to take care of my son as well as anyone else can.

August first, Uncle Steve's birthday, is Ethan's first party. He's five weeks old (Ethan, not my Uncle Steve) but really, considering when he *should* have been born it's more like he's one week old. Anyway, I go over to Christy's, give him his bath and dress him in his baseball outfit. He throws up all over it, so I give him another bath and put him in a clean sleeper.

I strap the carseat into my car, next to me, and then I strap Ethan into the carseat. I pack his diaper bag with bottles of formula, diapers, blankets, clean clothes. It's a major task. At the party, everyone makes cootchy-coo sounds over him. Babies make grown-ups look really stupid sometimes.

By September Ethan has learned to smile, make soft

little cooing sounds, and examine his feet and hands. I'm not sure if he's noticed his crooked fingers yet or not, but I keep showing them to him. Also, there's a special spot right under his chin which is like a smile button. If I just barely touch him there he breaks into this wide, toothless smile.

He sort of looks like me—not just his fingers, but the dimple in his chin, and maybe the shape of his face. His skin is kind of dark, like Christy's. I'm glad he's got her skin. Maybe he won't get acne like I did.

The evening of September eighth I stop by Christy's to say good-bye. Jeremy and I are taking off around midnight, hoping to get a lot of desert driving out of the way before noon tomorrow. Ethan is awake and happy. I pick him up and hold him, stretched out on my legs, so I can see his face.

"I'll miss you, little twerp," I tell him.

"Goo," he says back, with a smile.

I hold him and watch him for a long time, then put him on a blanket on the floor in the living room. He likes to be around people and noise. Christy walks out to my car with me.

"My dad doesn't want me to go back to school," she says. "He thinks I should stay home and take care of the baby."

"Your dad's nuts, Christy. You know that."

"But someone has to be responsible for the baby."

"Ethan's already got a spot reserved at the Infant Care Center," I remind her. "He can stay there during school hours. What's wrong with that?"

"Maybe they won't take care of him right."

"Christy, they're professionals. They'll probably take better care of him than we do."

"I don't know why I have to be the one to stay behind and take total responsibility. It's not fair," she says, beginning to cry.

"Lots isn't fair," I tell her. "It's not fair that you let

yourself get pregnant, either, god damn it!"

"I thought it would be different," she says in that kind of gasping way she gets when she cries.

"Well, it's not!"

"I know that!" she says, mad now. "I was so stupid! I thought you would love me more when I was pregnant with your baby, and that we'd live together at your house where people talk nice to each other. I know! I know! It was stupid! Why would I want to live with you anyway? You're selfish and you think you know everything. And I'll tell you something else, too, you don't even know how to make love right. Dashan showed me how good that could be!"

I just stand there, looking at her. "Finished?" I ask.

"I'm sorry you're my baby's father," she says.

"Yeah, well I'm not. I'm sorry I'm not older, so I could be a better father right now. But that's my kid in there and nothing's ever going to change that. Nothing. That was your decision in the beginning, and now you're stuck with it," I say, getting into my car.

I roll down the window and look straight into those green eyes that used to melt my heart. "You're not so great in bed, either, and I bet the big scar across your belly's not very attractive," I say as I slam the car into reverse and peel out of her driveway.

I drive straight to Jeremy's. "I'm ready to leave as soon as I pick up a few things back at the house," I say. "How about you?"

"Sure. I'll get my stuff. I've already delivered all living creatures but the snake to Stacy's house."

"What about the snake?"

"I sold Beatrice to the pet shop. Hated to do it, but I couldn't find anyone to snake-sit for four years."

We drive to my house and load up all my stuff. My mom and Steve and I went down to Barb and Edie's last night and had our last, for a long time, garbageburger. We talked for a very long time until Edie kept hanging around and we realized we were the last people in there and she wanted us to leave.

My mom says she wants to bring Ethan to our house about once a week so he won't forget her while I'm gone. And Steve says he's going to stop by and see the baby, too. I hope so. Maybe Ethan's so young it doesn't matter, but I want him to have more influences than just the Calderon family.

By the time I say good-bye to my mom again, and run across the street to say good-bye to Stacy, it's almost eleven. Mom and Stacy stand at the curb and wave to us as we head out for Texas. The trunk is filled with clothes, Jeremy's computer, and some of his favorite reference books. The backseat is full of more clothes, an ice chest, my portable CD player and my collection of favorite CDs. I also have an album of Ethan's baby pictures beginning with his first little preemie rat face up to the smiling, fat faced little guy in the polaroid picture I took earlier this evening, at Christy's, before the big blow-up.

At first I drive in silence, going over Christy's words in my head, thinking how much I'll miss Ethan, hoping he'll remember me when I see him next. And my mom. I feel inside my shirt pocket, being certain I didn't forget to bring the stamped postcards she handed me this evening. I'm supposed to drop one in the mail to her every night, or every four hundred miles, whichever comes first.

Jeremy has the big U.S. Atlas open on his lap. He's pointing his flashlight at Texas.

"When you drop me off at the Dallas/Fort Worth airport you'll probably only be about a hundred and fifty miles from Brooker University," he says. "Hey, we could stop at the Grand Canyon! Look, it's right here," he says, shoving the map in front of my face.

"Jeez, Jer! Are you trying to kill us?" I say, pushing the map away.

"Sorry . . . But it's practically on our way. Remember

that movie, *Grand Canyon*, with that black dude, what's his name?"

"Danny Glover."

"Yeah, that guy. He makes it sound like seeing the Grand Canyon is this amazing spiritual experience. We should go."

"*You're* wanting a spiritual quest? You don't even believe in God."

"Nature, my man. I believe in nature. Besides, it's time I found the meaning of life."

"I don't think anyone knows the meaning of life," I say.

"All the more reason for me to find it."

About three in the morning, somewhere in the Mojave Desert, I pull over to the side of the road. There's almost no traffic. It's not at all like the freeways we grew up with. Jeremy and I get out of the car and walk a little way from the shoulder, onto the sand, where we each take a leak. We go back to the car for the ice chest and start unloading sandwiches and sodas. Jeremy hands me one of those Handi-wipe things.

"What's this for?"

"The comforts of home, my man. Don't you usually wash after taking a leak?"

"Yes," I say, handing the package back to him. "But this time I didn't piss on my hands."

We sit eating, looking up at the stars. Jeremy points out and names constellations, but I just look up, amazed. The stars are never this bright at home. I've never seen such a bright night sky. It seems like there are about a million more stars overhead than there ever are in Southern California.

"You're a little quiet on this first night of Jeremy and Jeff's excellent adventure," Jeremy says.

I tell him about my last conversation, if you can call it that, with Christy.

"You can't take her seriously," Jeremy says. "She's not the most stable person in the world."

"But I have to take her seriously," I say. "She's the mother of my son. I can't exactly get her out of my life."

"I wouldn't be too worried about the effect her instability will have on Ethan."

"I wasn't worried about that at all, until you brought it up."

"Many truly great men had very unstable mothers . . . Look at Franklin Roosevelt. Look at Truman Capote."

"Very comforting," I say.

"And you're not going to fall for that old cliché about black guys being perfectly tuned sex machines, are you?"

"I don't even want to talk about it," I say.

"Remember, I roomed with Dashan in New Orleans."

"So?"

"So, I had plenty of opportunity to notice his equipment."

"And?"

"And, I'd say the two of you are about equally endowed in the sex machine department. And you *are* a better debate partner."

"Thanks," I say, sarcastically.

"Of course, I am purely virgin, but from what I hear and read, one's skills as a lover have more to do with the finesse with which one uses his tool than with the size of it."

I pack up the ice chest and put it back in the car. "Could we maybe change the subject?" I say.

"Sure. You're the one who brought it up."

"I did?" I say, thinking how tired I am. "Do you want to drive for a while, Jeremy?"

"Sure."

"I'm kind of sleepy, but if you're sleepy too, we could catch a nap before we start out again."

"Nope. I'm wide awake. We virgin guys have more stamina than you philanderers do."

"I'm hardly a philanderer," I say, leaning my head back against the seat and closing my eyes. It's been so long since I've had sex I could practically be designated a virgin myself. I don't know if Jeremy's really as pure as he says. He's had a few girlfriends over the course of his high school years. He may be telling the truth about virginity, or he may be following another of his old-fashioned codes, protecting a girl's reputation by hiding the fact that they had sex. Anyway, he says that abstinence is the wave of the future. He may be right.

I am lulled to sleep by the steady drone of the engine. I awaken when the car stops at a gas station and am surprised to see it's beginning to get light out. I stumble into the restroom, barely waking to do my thing. Jeremy comes in just as I'm washing up.

"Great. I'm glad to see you working on personal hygiene," he says.

"Where are we?"

"About forty miles out of Flagstaff," he says.

"Flagstaff? I don't remember Flagstaff when we mapped out our route."

"It's at the south end of the Grand Canyon," Jeremy says.

"But I didn't say we were going to the Grand Canyon."

"Well, I've almost got us there now. You know the old saying, you snooze, you lose."

"Jeremy!" I am now fully awake. I rush back to the car and grab the atlas.

"I've got it all figured out. We've got plenty of time to do this and get me to the airport in time. And if I miss my plane, well, I'll just take another. Spontaneity, my man, feeds the life force."

"Where are we?" I say, puzzling over the map.

"Highway 17, between Phoenix and Flagstaff," he says.

I groan. "God, Jeremy, we should be in Tucson, on our way to El Paso. Ten to 20, those were the only highways we needed to take."

"'You'll see. You'll like it. You'll thank me," Jeremy says, with this smug look on his face.

"Shit . . . How do other people end up deciding my life for

me? Christy decides to have *my* baby, you decide to drive *my* car to the Grand Canyon. Why don't I have a say in these decisions?"

"Good question, my man, good question."

As much as I know I'll miss Jeremy when we're living thousands of miles apart, I'm a little tired of him at this very instant.

CHAPTER

20

On the way in to Flagstaff, Jeremy tries to convince me to drive to the north rim.

"No! Damn it. We're going to the closest point and that's it."

"If we're going to see it, we should see it at its most impressive. We're only talking about another few miles."

I hang a U-turn and start back down Highway 17 toward Phoenix.

"No, no, no." Jeremy yells. "I'll be good, I promise. Please, please, please."

I turn around and head north again.

The sun is still low in the east when we get out of the car to look across the vast chasm. It is impossible to describe. Breathtaking? Awe-inspiring? Spectacular? Nothing says it. Perhaps breathtaking is best, because even Jeremy has to stop talking when he first sees it.

The layers of rock imbedded in the canyon walls are full of color—red, pink, black, orange, even bright lavender at places, along with the expected tones of sandstone and limestone. Huge towers of rocks jut out of the ancient earth. I know people have told me about this before, and I've half-listened. And I've seen it in the movies. But nothing has prepared me for this sight.

Finally Jeremy breaks the morning silence. "See what I've done for you, my man?"

"Thanks," I say, and I mean it. Then we get back in the Jetta and plan our route from Flagstaff to Dallas.

We stop around five at some generic Texas motel. It is over a hundred degrees outside and about sixty degrees in our room. I put the car keys deep inside my right front pocket and flop on my stomach on one of the twin beds. No way do I want Jeremy to be able to get my car keys. I loved seeing the Grand Canyon, but it would be just like him to decide on another side trip to Carlsbad Caverns, or who knows where.

In the morning I swim a few laps in the motel pool, shower, then go to the coffee shop for breakfast. Jeremy is already there, eating biscuits and gravy.

"Yuck," I say, looking at the mound of beige stuff on his plate.

"A Texas delicacy, my man. When one leaves one's own country, one should partake of the local cuisine."

I eat bacon and eggs, then we pack up and leave. I feel great! Free! My real life, my independent life, is about to begin. The sky is blue, the road stretches straight before us. I am on my way to becoming a new person.

At the Dallas/Fort Worth airport, I help Jeremy unload his stuff. We shake hands at the curb, wishing each other luck, and I drive off, looking for the highway that will take me south to Brooker Springs.

It is lonely at first without Jeremy, but soon my attention turns to the bright blue sky and the rolling green hills. How different this looks from home, how much clearer, and more expansive. But no sooner have I been awed by the blue sky than things turn gray, and heavy drops of rain pound down, making it hard to see through my windshield, even with the wipers going at high speed. And then, after fifteen minutes or so of this, all is clear again. Things don't happen that quickly in California—at least not weather kinds of things.

I get to within about five miles of Brooker University, but I keep having to stop and ask directions, and then something happens and I'm lost again. Finally, when I stop at the same little market for the third time, the old guy behind the counter unties his apron, hangs it by the door, flips the sign around so it says closed, and tells me, "Follow me, Son. Ah can tell you need a edacashun."

He gets into a beat-up old pick-up with a Texas license plate that says "T-R-U-C-K," and motions for me to follow him. After about a mile on the main drag of Brooker Springs, he turns right onto a narrow, unmarked road. It's not even exactly paved, it's just blacktop stuff. After another mile or so, he turns left into a driveway and there, past a row of pine trees, is a big old plantation style building with a sign in front that says Brooker University, Established 1882. My guide waves at me in his rear view mirror and completes the horseshoe-shaped drive that takes him back to the road.

I park and get out. It seems as if I've been in my car for about a year. I stretch and yawn and look up toward the big, white, columned building. A girl with long reddish hair is standing on the broad porch, watching me.

"Hi," she says.

"Hi."

"You here to register?"

"Yes."

"You're a long way from home," she says, eyeing my license plate.

"Yes. Are you a long way from home, too?" I ask.

"Nope. I grew up just over in Cotton County," she says, as if I would know where Cotton County is.

"Come on, I'll walk with you to registration."

"Okay." I reach into my car to get my wallet and the registration information I got in the mail about a month ago.

"I'm Jenny Sue Whitehead," the girl says, sticking her hand out.

"I'm Jeff," I say, reaching for the handshake. She has an amazingly firm grip.

"Jeff what?"

"Jeff Browning."

"Is that it? Your full name?"

"Jeffrey Dean Browning is my full name."

"Well, I'm pleased to meet you, Jeffrey Dean. You're in Texas now, Sugar, we like to use more than one name." She laughs, but I'm not sure if she's kidding or not.

The next few days pass in a whirl. I'm majoring in English with a communications minor. That's what Mr. Rogers advised. I've got two English classes, one modern American lit and one composition. I've got a P.E. class and, of course, debate. My debate teacher, Mr. Slokum, looks like he's about ninety years old. I hear he knows his stuff, but I don't think debate will be as much fun as it was with Rogers. I can't quite see driving Mr. Slokum nuts by singing "Ninety-nine Bottles of Beer on the Wall."

From my dormitory window I can see Lake Brooker. Absolutely everything around here is named after this Brooker guy who started the college. The lake isn't very big, but I guess it's big enough to contain a lot of fish because I see people fishing out there all the time.

My roommate, Kevin Brooker, (a distant relation of the founder of Brooker University) turns out to be Jenny Sue's fiancé. Several couples on this campus are "pinned." I don't think people go around pinning each other on the Cal State campuses. Maybe they do, but things seem different here. Anyway, I like Kevin, but he seems like the kind of guy who might only be able to get into a college founded by his great-great-great-grandfather.

There are about two thousand five hundred students enrolled at Brooker. That's about five hundred less than were at Hamilton High, so it seems small to me. And there are several buildings spread out over about ten acres, so it never seems crowded.

One of the first things I noticed in my classes was that the students here are mostly white. There are a few African-Americans, but no Asians, at least that I've seen so far, and no Latinos, either. That seems funny, for Texas. It took me a while to figure out what was missing, and then I realized—it was the variety of people and languages I've been used to seeing and hearing in California. I'm not complaining, really, it just seems strange.

We're already scheduled for a debate tournament the first weekend in October. I don't have a partner yet for Policy Debate. I want to see how things go before I get tied to someone who could end up being lazy, or difficult to work with. It's going to seem strange, doing that with anyone but Jeremy. This first tournament I'm only going to do Dramatic Interpretation. I wanted to do the section from *Roots,* the manhood section that Dashan used to do, partly because I understand it so much better now that I'm a father myself. But Mr. Slokum said not to do that—too ethnic he said. I don't understand his reasoning, but for now I'm just trying to go with the program.

J enny Sue and Kevin keep trying to set me up with some girl, but I tell them I'd rather find my own. One evening, while I'm sitting at my desk working on a paper for my composition class and Kevin is stretched out on his bed reading *Sports Illustrated,* he says, "Hey Jeff, there's something I need to talk with you about."

He looks so serious, I can't imagine what's on his mind.

"Shoot," I say.

"Well . . . You seem to be a healthy, red-blooded American boy. Why aren't you interested in girls?"

"I just haven't seen one to be interested in lately," I tell him. I could be interested in Jenny Sue, but I'm not stupid enough to say that to Kevin.

"You're not one of them California homo guys, are you?"

"No, Kevin, I like girls just fine," I say.

"Good. I know you're not from San Francisco, but I just had to ask anyway, 'cause I couldn't room with no faggot."

It's a good thing I'm getting acquainted with a lot more Texans than Kevin or I might end up with a very bad opinion of Texans.

One of the really great things about Brooker U. is that people are super friendly. Teachers, too. And I like my advisor a lot. He worked with me on a plan that will coincide with California Credential requirements, so when I'm ready to start teaching I'll be qualified in California as well as in Texas. I'm excited about that. I think I'll be good at it. Maybe not as good as Mr. Rogers, but probably better than Mr. Slokum.

When I see how the other debaters work, even the other two here on the same kind of scholarship I have, I realize what good training I got from Mr. Rogers. And he made it fun besides. That's the kind of teacher I want to be.

By November I've already won two dramatic interpretation events and took a third in an oratory event. Oratory is not really my thing. I only entered because I could do it alone. I still don't have a debate partner, although there's this girl, Nicole, who I might talk to about teaming up with me. It's strange. Even though I can do the debate stuff in front of people, sometimes it's hard for me to start talking with someone I don't know. It takes me a while to get acquainted.

I really like college. I like the people I *do* know so far, like Jenny and Kevin, and some of their friends. I'm living in a beautiful smog-free place and I don't even have to lock my car in the parking lot. But sometimes I get homesick, especially for Ethan. My mom wrote that he laughs now, and he can even roll over. I hope he still remembers me when I see him at Thanksgiving. I'm trading my unused New Orleans tickets for a round trip from Dallas to LAX.

Mom says I should wait for Christmas, but I don't want to. Besides, I'll drive home at Christmas. I know she'll say the weather is bad and it's dangerous, but that's what I plan to do anyway.

I miss my mom, and Steve, and Stacy, at home, and Benny and Jeremy and all my debate friends, but a lot of those people are gone from Hamilton Heights now anyway. And I know they'll remember me. Ethan is just a baby. I don't think his memory's very good yet.

21

After a month at B.U. I've got a routine I pretty much follow. Mondays, Wednesdays and Fridays I have classes from eight until twelve. Tuesdays and Thursdays debate meets from ten until twelve. In a way it's a very easy schedule, not like high school where you have to be in classes about thirty hours a week. Here it's more like sixteen hours a week. But there's a lot more reading to do and there aren't any weekly quizzes or homework assignments along the way. When it's time for mid-terms and finals, we have to know the material. No one is watching our progress.

I study in the library most afternoons, then go for a workout in the gym. Sometimes I get in on half-court basketball with some guys and afterwards we grab a drink together at the student union. One of the guys reminds me a little of Jeremy, always telling long, stupid jokes and using old-fashioned words. He makes me laugh. Some day I'll tell him the Patty Wack joke, but not yet.

I work at the student union about 15 hours a week. Compared to the 25 or 30 I used to put in at the Fitness Club, this is a cinch. Really, it's a great schedule. I have a lot more time to be spontaneous, but I don't always have spontaneous ideas.

The food in the student dining room is usually good, and I guess it's healthy if you consider cornbread one of the major food groups. I've never eaten so much cornbread in my life as I have the past month, but it's okay.

I miss garbageburgers, Mexican food and Thai food. Brooker Springs' contribution to exotic food is a hamburger place that has chop suey on the menu. Well, if I get desperate for a taste of Thailand I can probably drive to Dallas. A big city like Dallas must have everything.

Every evening after dinner I walk down by the lake. Kevin and Jenny Sue say I'm too much of a loner, but I've got a lot to think about. The wind in the pine trees and the gentle rippling of the water is soothing to me. I guess that having lived in a giant, sprawling city all my life, in the midst of smog and concrete, makes me appreciate being in a natural setting. At home we always had to drive to nature. Here it's like we're just in the middle of it.

There's a giant oak tree not far from the lake. It must be at least as old as the college. It's huge. I like to douse myself with mosquito repellent and sit under the tree, my back resting against the trunk. That's where I write letters home, when I write them.

Thursday evening I'm standing at the edge of the lake, trying to skip stones, when I hear a movement behind me. I jump. It's Nicole, from debate.

"Oops. I didn't mean to scare you," she laughs.

I laugh, too. "I was concentrating on my stone skipping technique and didn't know anyone else was around."

"Want company?"

"Sure."

She picks up a stone and throws it—five skips. Another—four skips.

"The most I can get is two," I say. "And that's about every eighth throw."

"I've had a lot of practice," she laughs.

I like her laugh. It's deep and free sounding. We stand

a few feet apart, throwing stones into the water, talking. She tells me a little about life in Tyler, Texas, where she grew up, and I tell her some about life in Hamilton Heights. Soon our talk turns to debate, since that's practically all we have in common.

"I did Policy Debate in high school," she tells me.

"Me, too."

"I don't want to start that here and get stuck with just any old partner."

"Me, either," I admit.

"I've been thinking about you," she says.

"I've been thinking about you . . . So that settles it then," I say.

"Are you sure?"

"Pretty sure," I laugh.

"Tell me more about life in California."

"Like what?"

"Tell me the glamorous parts."

Now I really laugh.

"It is glamorous!" she says. "I watch the Academy Awards every year, and then the party at Spago. You can't tell me it's not glamorous."

"You know that movie, *Grand Canyon?*"

"No."

"Well you should watch it. It says a lot about life in California."

"If it's about the Grand Canyon what's that got to do with California?"

"You just have to see it."

"So show me."

"I will," I say.

Nicole and I spend much of the weekend in the library, gathering facts and statistics for Policy Debate. We work well together. She doesn't have that photographic memory thing like Jeremy does, but she's much better organized and that makes up for it.

Monday we stop by Slokum's office and ask him to sign

us up as a team for the next tournament.

"Good, you'll do well together," he says. And that's it.

When we teamed up with Rogers, he'd ask all kinds of questions about how we were gathering information, who would be in what role as a partner, how we were organizing statistics. With Slokum we're totally on our own.

I like Nicole. She's as easy to talk and laugh with as my old friend, Stacy, but she's more than that. I watch for her on campus now, and when I see her, my heart beats faster.

Our first tournament as a team is in Dallas. We don't make it into the Finals, but we come close. It's a good beginning.

"Come on," I say. "We're in Big D. Let's go find a great Thai food restaurant."

"What's that?" she says.

"You know, like they eat in Thailand—mint and chili chicken, spicy peanut sauce, red curry rice."

She gives me a blank look.

"I'm starving for spicy," I tell her.

"I know a great Mexican food place," she says. "My sister lives here and sometimes, when I visit, we go to this great place called Stevie's."

"Stevie's?"

"All I can say is it's got great food."

"Okay. Mexican sounds good, too."

We get in my car and start driving around.

"We're close. I know we're close," she keeps saying. "Turn left!"

I cut across lanes to the sound of blaring horns and turn left, onto a dead-end street.

"Oh, this must be Stevie's," I say, pointing to the iron gate which blocks the entrance to a junkyard.

"Calm down, calm down," she says. "Now I know exactly where we are."

"Why don't I believe you?"

"No, really. Go back up this street."

I follow her directions and then, after eight or nine

circuitous blocks, she tells me to stop.

"But Nicole, there's nothing here but apartments. You promised me Mexican food," I say.

"This is where my sister lives. She'll tell me how to get there. Come on up and say hi," she says.

I'm not wild about this side trip to meet Nicole's sister, but I'm stuck now. We walk up the steps and see mail and newspapers piled up on the porch. At first Nicole looks puzzled, then remembers that her sister is in the Bahamas on a ten-day cruise she won for selling the most cars at the dealership where she works.

"Your sister's a car salesman?"

"Yeah, and my brother's a decorator. So what?"

"So nothing," I laugh. "Don't get all paranoid on me. I was just asking."

She laughs, too. "My dad always makes such a big deal of it, like couldn't they just switch jobs or something—I guess I get kind of protective of them."

Nicole fumbles around under a potted plant, pulls out a key and opens the door. She gathers up the newspapers and mail and walks inside.

"Come on in," she says, putting the papers on the kitchen counter and writing a note to her sister:

> "Dear Katie—My debate partner and I stopped by to get directions to Stevie's. I forgot you were off on a luxury liner. Hope you're having a great time! Love you—Nick

"Great apartment," I say. The living room has high ceilings and huge front windows that give a view of the Dallas skyline. Bright colored dramatic paintings of things I can't identify hang on the other two walls.

"State of the art sound system, too," Nicole says, opening double doors which conceal a complete stereo system and a giant TV screen.

I check out the titles on some of the hundreds of compact disks which are neatly shelved next to the stereo unit.

"Nice CD collection," I say.

"I'm sure Katie would be happy to know you approve," Nicole laughs.

It turns out that Nicole can figure out how to get to Stevie's now that she's in her sister's familiar neighborhood. We pig out. It's a different kind of Mexican food than I'm used to in California. I guess it's what they call Tex-Mex. But it's good.

All along our plan has been to go back to B.U. after dinner.

"I'm having such a good time, I don't want to go back to school yet, do you?" I ask Nicole.

"No," Nicole says. She has deep brown eyes, but sometimes they get almost a yellow light in them, and then I think maybe she has some special feelings for me, too.

"Remember the first day we talked at the lake, and I promised to show you that movie *Grand Canyon*, so you'd stop bugging me with questions about California?"

"Bugging you! I wasn't bugging you, I was trying to draw you out. You seemed like such a lonely guy."

"Anyway," I laugh, trying to sound more casual than I feel, "do you think your sister would mind if we watched that video at her place? I'm sure we could find it in any video store."

Nicole looks at me a long time as I nonchalantly move beans from one side of my nearly empty plate to the other. Finally she says, "I'm sure Katie wouldn't mind, as long as we don't mess things up."

"I promise to be as neat as Mary Poppins," I say, grinning.

We leave the restaurant and find a video store about a block away. They have the movie we're looking for. We buy some microwave popcorn and Cokes for later and head back toward her sister's apartment. My mind is racing. I don't think anything is really going to happen. We've never even kissed. We lean next to each other and touch shoulders sometimes when we're working in the library. We really are only friends. Still . . .

"Sometimes I get these monstrous headaches when I watch a movie," I lie. "I'm going to stop at this drugstore up here and run in for some aspirin."

"I'm sure Katie has aspirin," Nicole says.

"Yeah, well, I always use a certain kind," I tell her as I turn into the drugstore parking lot. "Be right back," I say, jumping from the car and sprinting to the entrance, praying she doesn't decide she needs something, too, and follow me in. Where are they? Where are they? Finally I spot them and grab a three-pack of condoms, checking to be sure they've got the lubricated tip.

On my way to the cashier I decide I'd better get some aspirin. How stupid that would be! I make my purchases, slip the condom package in my inside jacket pocket and leave the aspirin in the bag. When I get back in the car, Nicole checks the bag.

"These are just plain old aspirin. I thought you needed a special kind."

"No," I say, thinking fast. "I need the plain old kind but I bet your sister only has specialized aspirin. Besides, I'd hate to take her last two and then have her come home from her vacation, late at night, with a splitting headache, and find no aspirin left in her supply. Maybe she'd have a hangover, or . . . "

"Okay, okay," Nicole laughs. "Enough about the damned aspirin."

Back at the apartment we put the tape in the VCR and stretch out on the floor, close but not touching, our heads propped against giant pillows, and start the tape.

"Why is that helicopter always flying around like something out of Vietnam? Is that supposed to be some big symbol of something?"

"I don't know. There's always police helicopters flying around out there. I could hardly sleep the first few nights in the dorms because it was so quiet. No helicopters, no sirens, no gunshots."

"You're kidding, right?"

"No."

"Where you live?"

"Yeah."

"God. That's awful!"

"Watch the movie," I say.

Somewhere about half-way through the movie, when Danny Glover and his new friend, Jane, I think, are falling in love, Nicky moves her head over and rests it on my chest. When the two teenagers are kissing good-bye after camp, I reach up and stroke her hair. It's soft and fine feeling. I look down at my hand, stroking her hair, and think how blond her hair is, how I like how it looks as I move my fingers through it.

When the movie is over we lie close, talking for a long time. She tells me there's no such thing as gangs where she grew up. I tell her about the kid who was shot last year, two blocks from Hamilton High. And about the kid who was caught with a gun on campus. She tells me about how some kids were caught drinking beer in her high school parking lot.

"Maybe there was a lot going on there that you didn't know about," I say.

"I'd know if there were police helicopters flying over my house when I was trying to sleep, and if some kid was shot near my school. I'm surprised all the good people haven't left L.A."

"One of them did," I say, gently tipping her head up and kissing her on the lips.

"Um, I'm glad one of them did," she murmers, returning my kiss.

She puts her head back on my shoulder. "Really, why would anyone stay there?"

"It's L.A. There's a lot going on—music, theater, film, sports, skiing, surfing, lots of good colleges. Besides, why should the good people leave and let the bad people take over? Good and bad, it's not that simple, you know, but I think good people have to hang in there."

"I hope this good person hangs in here for a while," she says, kissing me again. This kiss is longer, more serious. I touch her lips with my tongue and she parts them, slightly. My mind is saying don't rush things, don't rush things, but my body is straining toward her, urgently wanting more. I kiss her neck, her throat, she takes my head between her two hands and holds my face in front of hers, inches away, stopping my kisses.

"What are we doing?" she asks in a whispery voice.

"Getting better acquainted?"

"How much better?"

"Much, much better, I hope."

I kiss her again, pulling her close. Head to toe, our bodies touch. I slip my hand under her blouse, feeling her warm softness. "God, I love the feel of your skin," I say.

She moves her hand along the inside of my thigh. I think I will burst.

"Nicole. Oh, God, Nicole."

"Wait," she says. "Wait."

She moves quickly into the other room and when she returns she is wearing a robe, open in front. God, she is beautiful. I've got my shirt off and my pants unbuttoned. She lies back down beside me, close. I reach for the condom I already took from the package while she was out of the room. When she sees it she says, "Don't worry with that. I'm on the pill."

I kiss her again, caress her body where I know she wants to be caressed. When she whispers, "Come on, come on," I again reach for the condom. "Don't you trust me when I say I'm on the pill?" she asks, pulling slightly away.

"I trust you. But I don't trust the pill," I say, pulling her close again.

"You don't have some California disease, do you?" she whispers, leaning close against my body, moving her leg over mine.

"No. You don't have some Texas disease, do you?" We both laugh, and then we get very serious.

I awake early in the morning, my arms around Nicole, her head resting on my chest. God, I like feeling close to her, body to body. And not just the body stuff either. I never get tired of her humor, or her conversation. I feel great this morning, until Christy's words come back to me, telling me I'm not a good lover. Maybe that hurt me more than I cared to think about at the time. Not that I'm trying to be any macho stud or anything, but no guy likes to think he's a klutz in bed.

Nicole stirs and I kiss the top of her head. "Good morning," I say.

"Mornin' Sunshine," she says in her most exaggerated Texas drawl.

"Nicky . . . " I start. I want to ask her if I was okay in bed, but I can't figure out how to say it without sounding dumb.

She wriggles closer to me. "I liked last night," she says, planting quick kisses on my lips, cheeks, forehead.

"Really?"

"Really, for certain, for sure."

We lie together for a few moments, under a fluffy down comforter, as sunlight filters through the room's gauzy curtains.

"I've only done this with one other guy in my whole life," she says.

"Want to tell me about it?" I ask.

"Umm. Not right now I guess." She moves her lips to mine and we are very quickly ready to do what we did last night.

"It's a good thing I bought a three-pack," I say, feeling her body close against me.

"Yeah, Jeffrey Dean," she laughs. "A boy's always got to have aspirin on hand."

CHAPTER

22

Most couples have their own special song, but with me and Nicole it's a movie—*Grand Canyon*. We've already watched it twice since the first time in Dallas. I don't want to say I love her yet, because we've only known each other such a short time. But I do love her, whether I'm saying it or not. She makes me smile all over when I see her walking toward me, or when I watch her practicing a debate presentation.

I don't exactly know how to tell Nicole about Ethan. Not that I'm ashamed of him, or that we're making lifetime plans or anything, but we got very close very fast. I don't go blurting my personal story out the first week I meet people. But then, after that night at her sister's place, it seemed like maybe I'd been hiding something from her. So I ask to meet her by the lake after dinner. We stand at the same place we stood a few weeks ago, skipping rocks. I'm getting better, but not much.

"There's something I want to tell you," I say.

Her eyes widen, and she stands very still. "You're sorry you got involved with me," she says.

I pull her toward me. "No. Never . . . There are just some things I want you to know."

Then I tell her about Ethan, and Christy, and how I want to be a better dad than HANK 40 has been. She's very quiet through it all, then asks to see pictures of Ethan. We walk to the dorms and I get the album from my top dresser drawer. She sits on the edge of the bed, checking him out. In one of the pictures, Christy is holding Ethan. Nicole looks at Christy for a long time before she turns the page.

"He looks like you," she says. "Is he healthy now?"

"He seems to be," I say. "The doctor says some things don't show up at first. Like he could have trouble learning when he gets to school. Or maybe he won't be very well coordinated—it's too soon to know about some things."

"Poor little guy," she says.

We sit looking at the latest picture of Ethan for a long time, each thinking our own thoughts.

"Okay, my turn," she sighs. "You know I told you I'd only ever been with one other guy?"

I nod. Is she going to tell me she's had hundreds? That she was a slut all through high school?

"We're still sort of engaged," she says.

"Engaged?"

"Well, not exactly, but everyone expects us to get married some day, including him. We've been together since junior high school."

"Do *you* expect to marry him?"

"I used to think that. Now I'm not so sure," she says, not meeting my eyes.

"What do you think now?"

She looks up at me. "I think I've never felt so strongly about anyone in my life, and I want to be in bed with you right now. But I don't want to hurt Donny. I thought I loved him until I met you, and now I can hardly remember what he looks like."

"Well . . . one day at a time?" I ask.

She nods.

"Let's work on the part about how you want to be in bed with me right now," I say, pulling her toward me.

Just as we're locked in a heated embrace, our hands all over each other, Kevin walks in. He takes one look at us, says "Thank God," and walks back out again.

Neither of us wants to be separated at Thanksgiving break, but it's been over two months since I've seen Ethan. I can hardly recognize him in the picture I got from Mom yesterday. I try to talk Nicole into coming home with me.

"It's a chance to see glamorous Los Angeles," I tell her.

"Somehow that idea isn't as appealing to me as it once was. I can skip the police copters flying over my Thanksgiving turkey, and bullets whizzing around the street. You come home with me."

"And face Donny?" I laugh.

"We've both got to go to our own homes," she says, getting suddenly serious. "You know I'd follow you to the ends of the earth, police copters and all. But I've got to figure some things out and let Donny know where things stand. And you've got to see your baby so he doesn't forget you . . . It's only for five days," she reminds me.

The week before I leave for L.A. I write to Christy.

Dear Christy, I'll be home the Wednesday before Thanksgiving Day. The main reason I'm flying home is to see Ethan. I'd like to visit him Wednesday evening, and then take him to my house for a few hours on Thursday. I'm sorry we parted on such unfriendly terms. I want to try to get along with you so Ethan can love us both without feeling like he has to choose sides. I think we both want what's best for him.

I sign the letter sincerely, because I do honestly, sincerely, hope we can get along for the sake of our son.

When Nicole and I say good-bye, before I get on the airport bus, she gives me a postcard with a picture of the

Grand Canyon on front. On the back it says, "Remember me." I hand her a CD that includes "The Grand Canyon Suite," which is what they play on the Disneyland train trip, and I've signed my name across the front of the cover with a gold metallic pen. Neither of us has used the word love with the other. There are tears in her eyes as she waves good-bye, and tears in mine, too. I wonder if she will love Donny again when she sees him?

On the flight home I read from *The Autobiography of Mark Twain,* which is an assignment for modern American lit. Somehow Mark Twain doesn't strike me as modern, but the professor teaching the class looks like he might have been traveling the river with Twain when he was a young man, so maybe it's modern to him. Modern or not, it's interesting and it helps the flight go quickly.

Mom and Steve and Stacy are waiting to meet me as I fight my way through the crowds of people at LAX. They all attack me at once, laughing and hugging. For a moment I forget the love I've left in Texas, I'm so happy to be with the people I love here.

On the way home they bombard me with questions about school and Brooker Springs. Have I met new friends? Do I like Texas? How's debate? How's the weather? How's my room? My roommate? And on and on, so fast I can hardly answer them.

"How's Ethan?" I ask.

"He's doing fine," Mom says. "You won't recognize him."

"I want to see him as soon as we get home," I say.

"Okay," Mom says. "Then how about all of us going to Barb and Edie's?"

I groan in happy anticipation. "You don't know how much I've missed those garbageburgers. And onion rings."

"You don't look like you're hurting for food," Steve says, punching me in the belly."

"Hey, show me you can button these pants around your gut—then your insulting remarks might mean something."

We all laugh. I've missed these people so much. I wish

Nicole were here with me, getting to know the people I love.

I've brought a Brooker University teddy bear for Ethan. I
wind it up so it's playing the alma mater as I walk to the
door of Christy's house. Her mom answers the door and
invites me in. Mr. Calderon is sitting in his E-Z Boy rocker,
watching TV, with Ethan asleep on his shoulder. I walk
over and stand looking down at him.

"Getting big, huh?" Mr. Calderon says, smiling.

I can hardly believe it's the same baby. He's chubby! I
reach down and touch his hand—check out his crooked
pinkies. He stirs a bit but doesn't waken. Mr. Calderon
says, "I think he'll stay asleep for awhile. Why don't you
put him in his crib?"

I reach down for Ethan and lift him to my shoulder,
being careful to support his head. But he's strong now.
Even though he's sound asleep, he's not all wobbly. I lay
him in his crib, propped on his side the way I first learned
when he was in the hospital. I cover him with a light
blanket and go back to the kitchen where Mrs. Calderon is
making tamales. I wash my hands and start helping her
put them together, as I did two years ago at Thanksgiving,
when everything was different.

"Where's Christy?"

"None of your business," Maria yells from her bedroom.

"Hello, Maria," I yell back.

She comes in, smiling. "Hey, Homes," she says.

She looks tough. She's dressed like a Chola, wearing
black eye make-up and plenty of it. I guess she's thirteen
now. I'm not sure. She hangs around the kitchen for a
while, then goes back to watch TV.

"That girl's going to kill me if she doesn't straighten up,"
Mrs. Calderon says. "She's been sent home from school
three times already. Three!"

"Why?"

"Gang attire. She dresses right at home but somewhere

between here and school she changes clothes . . . We *never* had such problems with Christina . . . Well, but maybe Maria won't get pregnant so young . . . I don't think I could take another one. I love little Ethan, but you know, babies are a lot of work and I'm not so young anymore."

We concentrate on the tamales for a while, not talking, and then I ask again, "Where's Christy?"

"She's working at The Gap, down at the mall. She'll be home by nine, unless she goes out with the girls from work for a while."

"How many days a week does she work?" I ask.

"Oh, most. She and Ethan get home from the Infant Center around three and she usually needs to be at work by four."

"Hey, Mom," Maria yells from the living room. "The rug rat is crying!"

I go back to Christy's room and pick up the baby. He doesn't smell very good. I turn on the light and reach for a diaper. Everything's in the same place it was the last time I was here—diapers, baby wipes, burp cloths.

I undo his dirty diaper, being careful to put the clean one over him so he won't pee on me. I learned that the hard way when he was first out of the hospital. I clean his butt, which is about twice the size it was when I last saw it, and fasten his clean diaper. Then I pick him up. He's got eyebrows and eyelashes and even some hair. He no longer looks like a baby skinhead.

"Wow! You are one big guy," I say.

He grabs a hunk of my hair and pulls. "Hey! When did you learn that trick?" I unwrap his fingers from my hair and hold him cradled in my arm, so I can see his face. He looks at me for a long time. I don't think he remembers me, but then I find the smiling spot under his chin and his face lights up. Maybe he does remember me.

"Remember me?" I say. "I'm your daddy." I tell him how I first saw him in the hospital. I show him how my fingers and his look the same. He watches everything, and listens.

Mrs. Calderon comes in and stands beside us.

"He looks great," I say. "Someone's taking good care of him."

"Christy and I take good care of him," she says. "Christy's a good mother, but, you know—seventeen. She doesn't always want to be tied down. Alfredo watches out for him, too—holds him and feeds him. I didn't think he'd be like that, but he is. Life surprises us sometimes, doesn't it?"

I nod, then suddenly I notice the tee shirt Ethan is wearing. "Hey. What's this Cal Berkeley stuff?"

"Dashan sent him that," Maria yells from the living room, as if she's been listening to every word.

"Dashan's always sending something," Mrs. Calderon says.

I don't say anything. It's nice, I guess, that Dashan sends him shirts but I'd rather see Ethan in a Brooker University shirt. Of course, that would be difficult, since I haven't sent him one. I will as soon as I get back to school.

"Look at your teddy bear," I say, taking the bear and winding the key. "Listen." I make the bear dance to the music and Ethan lets out a big laugh. God, I love this little boy. I want him always to have a good life. I don't want anything, ever, to hurt him.

Thanksgiving Day I get Ethan and take him back to my house. It's the usual crowd for dinner, with one addition—Douglas, the guy who graduated from nursing school with my mom. I notice he's at home in our kitchen—knows where to find everything and helps himself to a beer from the fridge. Once, when he brushes close to my mom as she's basting the turkey he looks into the oven. "Nice breast," he says, then raises one eyebrow in a way that makes me think he's admiring more than the turkey. My mom laughs. What's going on here?

Just as I'm about to dig into my mashed potatoes, complete with a well of turkey gravy, Ethan starts to cry.

I hope he'll stop, but he doesn't. I take one quick, delicious mouthful, put down my fork and pick him up from the couch where he's been sleeping. I hold him and pat him, but he keeps crying. It's only been an hour since I gave him a bottle, so he can't be hungry. I change him and rock him. He still cries.

"What should I do?" I ask my mom.

"I don't know. Sometimes babies just need to cry."

"Let me try," Douglas says.

I hand Ethan over, and Douglas walks with him from room to room. It doesn't work. His lungs must be pretty strong now, 'cause he's making a very big sound. I call Christy's house. She answers the phone. It's the first time I've talked to her since I left for Texas.

"Hi," I say.

"Jeff?"

"Yeah. I can't get the baby to stop crying," I tell her. "What should I do?"

"Is he hungry? Wet? Have you tried rocking him?"

I assure her that we've tried it all.

"Well . . . Sometimes I take him for a ride in the car when nothing else works."

I hang up, wrap Ethan in a blanket, put his hat on him, take him to my car and strap him into his seat. His face is red and he's screaming at the top of his lungs. It's awful! I start the car and drive slowly down the street. I've driven two blocks when Ethan stops crying. In another two blocks he's asleep. I drive, aimlessly, past old familiar sights—the street where Christy and I used to always park, the Fitness Club, Hamilton High School. I turn down Benny's street and see his car in the driveway so I stop and ring the doorbell.

"Is Benny home?" I ask his dad.

"Jeff. Come in," he says, grabbing my hand and giving it an enthusiastic shake.

"I can't. I've got the baby in the car," I say. "Where's Benny?"

"Basic Training," Mr. Dominguez says. "Maybe it'll straighten him out."

He walks with me to my car and looks in at Ethan. "Benny told me you and Christy had a baby. I guess your carefree days are over now, huh?"

"I guess so," I say, getting back in my car. "Tell Benny hi for me next time you talk to him."

I drive by Jeremy's, even though I know he's not home, and Dashan's, and Trin's, but I know they're all away at school, at least until Christmas.

Ethan is still sound asleep when I get back to my house. I carry him carefully into the living room and put him back down on the couch. He barely moves.

Everyone is in the den now, watching the game and eating pumpkin pie.

"I saved a plate of food for you," Mom says.

I put my plate in the microwave and eat my warmed-up dinner. Before I finish my pie, Ethan is crying again.

"I'll get him," Mom says.

"He's probably hungry now," I say.

Douglas warms a bottle and mom holds Ethan, watching him while he eats. "I love the feel of his furry little noggin," she says, rubbing her hand lightly across the top of his head. When Ethan stops eating she hands him to Douglas, who holds him against his shoulder and rubs his back until this loud burp erupts.

"You're going to have to teach this kid some manners," Steve says.

"I thought that's what great-uncles did," I tell him.

"Nope. Great-uncles only play."

I take Ethan back to Christy's about ten.

"Can I come get him tomorrow?" I ask her.

"Sure. I have to work, and my mom can use a break, I guess."

I hand Ethan over to Christy, carry all his stuff from the car into her room, say goodnight and leave. Christy and I still don't talk much, except about the baby.

23

"**J**eff! Over here!"

I am surprised to see Nicole waving to me as I get off the plane in Dallas. I run to her and hug her tight. She kisses me, laughing.

"Daddy let me borrow his car until Christmas," she says, leading me to a brand new Cadillac parked in valet parking. "I decided to swing by the airport and meet you."

I put the seat in a reclining position and breathe in the new car smell.

"How did you get him to let you keep this for a month?"

"By being his darlin' baby girl," she says with a smile. "Besides, he's going to Hong Kong on business next week and probably won't be back much before Christmas."

I ask the question that's been on my mind for the past five days. "How did things go with Donny?"

Nicole frowns. "Not so good, at first. He was upset. Very upset."

"What did you tell him?"

"The truth."

"Which is?"

"That I've met someone, things have happened, and I want to be free to follow my feelings. We parted friends, sort of—how about Baby Ethan?"

"He's practically grown," I say.

"How was California?"

"Different. Noisy. Crowded. I'm glad to be on my way to Brooker Springs."

We talk, sitting in Nicole's dad's car in front of the dorms, until sunrise. When Kevin leaves for his eight o'clock class, Nicky and I sneak into my room and use my bed for more than sleeping.

I do a lot of thinking after Thanksgiving. When it's not raining, and sometimes even when it is, I sit leaning against the broad trunk of the huge old oak tree, looking toward the lake, and thinking about my life. I know I want to teach. I want to be someone who reaches others. And I want to stay in the debate program here at B.U. Debate makes me think. Part of me falls asleep when I'm not involved with debate—like the whole dramatic side of me goes into hibernation.

I often sit under the oak tree, thinking the same thoughts over and over, because of Ethan. And, even though I don't believe in ghosts, that Kunta Kinte talk from *Roots* practically haunts me—how it is the job of the father to be as a giant tree to his manchild. This oak tree I sit under shelters me from rain or sun, supports me as I lean against it. Roots, trunk, branches, leaves—substances of life. How can I be as a giant tree to my son, when I am, myself, sitting under a giant tree in Brooker Springs, Texas?

By December, just before the end of first semester, I can finally make most stones do about three hops to Nicky's five. We are throwing stones, and talking.

"Nicky . . ."

She stops and looks at me, frowning. She can tell in an instant if I'm joking or serious.

"Nicky . . ."

"You're moving back to California," she says.

I throw another stone. It sinks. We watch its ripples broaden and diminish.

"Tell me you're not moving back to California."

"I've got to, Nick. Come with me. California has schools, too."

"I knew it," she says, turning to face me.

"How could you? I just figured it out myself."

"Texan's intuition," she says, laughing, then comes over to me and hugs me hard.

"Every time I see a kid with his dad, or hear the D.I. piece that guy from Carson does, I get a pain in my chest that goes clear through to my backbone. I can't only see my son at vacation times. I want to be more than a vacation dad. He deserves more," I say, kissing her. "Come with me. I don't want to lose you. I need you."

She pulls away.

"I can't just tag along after you, Jeff."

"I want you near me so we can love each other. Don't you want that?"

"Yes. You know I do. But I want it here. This is my school. I've planned to come here since I was a little girl. My mother and father met here. I want to love you here," she says, then picks up a stone, skips it seven times, turns and walks away.

I skip stones until my arm feels like lead. Nothing changes in my mind, though. I've thought it through. I have to be near Ethan, day by day, not just now and then. As much as I love Nicky, I've got to leave this place because if I don't, someday a few years down the road Ethan's probably going to be calling someone else daddy, and I'll end up with about as much respect for myself as I now have for HANK 40.

I find Dr. Slokum in his office and tell him I'm leaving at the end of this semester.

"Oh, no, Jeff. You're doing so well. I was talking with Dean Walters about you just last week. I can almost assure you of four years of full scholarship if you stay."

"I can't," I say. I try to explain about Ethan, but I don't think he gets it. "I'm sorry," I tell him.

The next weeks are taken up with finishing term papers, studying for finals, and Nicky. We both pretend not to be counting the days, but it doesn't take any Texas intuition to know that we are. The night before I'm to leave, as the Jetta sits packed and ready in the parking lot, Nicky and I lie together in the soft leather back seat of her father's Cadillac, parked off a narrow dirt road under pine trees wet from a recent rainstorm. Nicky grabs hold of my ears, pulling my face to hers, kissing me fiercely, then pushing me away.

"Why did we love each other so much, so fast?" she says. "Why did you make me love you?"

"I didn't make you love me. It was a gift," I say.

"What do you mean?"

"The same force that gave us the Grand Canyon, and music, and shooting stars, and trees, and sent Ethan my way—that force gave us these months. Come to California with me. Let's not throw away our gift."

"I can't," she sighs. "You know how you're afraid you won't respect yourself if you're not a good father to Ethan?"

"Yeah."

"Well, I'm afraid I won't respect myself if I don't follow through on my Brooker University dream."

"You said you'd follow me to the ends of the earth," I remind her.

She looks at me for a long time. "It's a figure of speech," she says.

"And you said you loved me," I say.

"That's a reality."

So here I am, back in Hamilton Heights, living with my mom again, attending community college, and working at the Fitness Club. I found a used crib, which I cleaned up and put in my room. Ethan is with me Sunday through

Tuesday, and with Christy Wednesday through Friday. We each have him every other Saturday. It's working out. He knows me now, no doubt about that.

When I walk through the door at Christy's house he squeals and moves his arms up and down. When I pick him up he nuzzles his head in the place between my neck and shoulder.

He goes to the Infant Center, which is part of Hamilton High's Teen Parent Program, every school day, unless he's sick. He's sick a lot, mostly with little stuff, but the doctor says that's common with preemies. When he can't go to the Infant Center we have to scramble to find someone to take care of him. Sometimes Christy or I miss school on those days.

Sometimes Christy's mom takes care of him, but she's been kind of sick a lot herself. When my mom works from midnight to eight, it's hard for her to come home and start taking care of Ethan right away. But her friend, Douglas, stayed with Ethan one day last week, when he had a fever and couldn't go to Infant Care. And Uncle Steve stayed with him last Sunday when I had to work at the Fitness Club.

When I look at all the time and work and people it takes for this one baby, it reminds me of the persuasive speech Dashan gave during tournaments our junior year. It had to do with how it takes a whole village to raise a child. That saying is almost a cliché now. I even saw it on a coffee cup that Mrs. Bergstrom, the Infant Care teacher, was using. But the first time I heard the whole village thing was from Dashan. It made sense to me then, in theory, but now it's a reality. Lots of people are part of raising Ethan, but I'm one of the biggest parts of all. I like that. It feels right to me.

Here's my plan now. I'll finish two years at Hamilton Heights City College, then transfer to a four-year state school, either L.A., or Cal Poly.

Since I'm now in school without a scholarship, and Ethan always needs stuff that costs money, I have to work a lot of hours just to make ends meet. Also, my telephone bill to Nicole is always very high. So it's hard to go to school full-time. It's probably going to take about six years to get my teaching credential. I hope I can hang.

H.H.C.C. doesn't have a debate program. I miss that a lot—the excitement that comes with competitions, and the closeness that develops among debaters. Mr. Rogers called when he heard I was back in town and invited me to be a judge at the next tournament. That'll be fun, but it won't be the same as competing. Truthfully, college seems dull without debate. And another thing, H.H.C.C. is on a noisy, busy street. It's always hard to find a place to park, and there's no lake, or trees.

On days when there are warnings about the air being unhealthful I want to put Ethan in the car and head for Brooker Springs. But I know it wouldn't work. Here are some of the people who love Ethan: Me, of course, and Christy. Mrs. Calderon and even Mr. Calderon and little tough-chick Maria. My mom, Steve, Douglas, Stacy and Dashan. I guess Dashan, 'cause he keeps sending Ethan Berkeley shirts and sweats. Anyway, that's at least ten people, plus Bergie in Infant Care. In Texas there would only be me and Nicole.

I know Nicole would love him, but I'm not sure she'd want to take care of him when he's sick. So I know it's just a fantasy to think about running away with Ethan. Not to mention that Christy would have the FBI out after us if we even got close to a state border.

In spite of Christy not wanting to see Ethan after he was first born, I think she loves him a lot. He's really changed her life, though. She dropped debate because it takes up too much time on weekends, and she needs to work to help support Ethan, too. She's still working as an aide in the Hearing Impaired program.

I think she and Dashan are just friends now. That's

what he told me the last time I saw him. He and I are planning a reunion with the debate group this summer. It was Dashan's idea. He's missing the old crowd even more than I am.

It's funny about Dashan. All through high school he was about the most popular, successful guy you could imagine—super nice, smart, but never conceited about any of it. But he's having a hard time in college.

"It's so big," he says. "It's like I'm nothing."

"You should see the Grand Canyon," I tell him.

"That's different," he says.

"Do you ever run into Trin up there?"

"Yeah. She's practically the only one I talk to. I see her about once a week or so."

I just sit there looking at his sad face. I can't believe it. The most together guy I've ever known, and he's worse off than I am. Things really change after high school.

I sort of want to ask Dashan about him and Christy. Are they friends, or more than friends? I think I'm curious mainly because of what Christy said to me that time, about me not knowing how to make love. Man, that nagged at me for a while. I think she was so mad that day she would have said anything she could think of to hurt me. Besides, I know Nicole was very happy with me in that department, and that's what matters. But it's not really my business what goes on between Dashan and Christy, so I don't ask.

Here's something strange, though. For a while, when Benny was home on leave after Basic Training, he and Christy were seeing each other. From Dashan to Benny is a big leap. I mean, Benny is a nice guy, except at times when he's drinking, but I'm surprised Christy was interested in him. I don't care who Christy's with, but I do care who's driving my son around.

When I first heard that Benny and Christy were seeing each other, I could imagine Benny taking Christy and Ethan to the beach, drinking beer all day, and then driving them home, drunk, on the freeway. So I stopped by his house one day, and I just told him straight out, "Don't be drinking and then drive around with Ethan in your car."

"Hey, thanks, Dad," Benny said, all sarcastic.

"I mean it, Benny."

"Lighten up, will you? You worry too much."

"I want you to tell me you won't drive with Ethan in the car if you've been drinking."

He just stood looking at me for a long time, hard like. Then he said, "Okay. Okay. My leave's almost over anyway."

We went into Benny's garage and played pool for a while. We talked about army life, and H.H.C.C. I told him about how Jeremy managed to trick me into seeing the Grand Canyon and we had a good laugh over Jeremy and old times. When I left, Benny shook my hand and said, "Hey, Man. I'm always sober when I see Christy and the baby. I wouldn't do anything to hurt your kid."

"Thanks, Ben," I told him.

I know he was right. I worry too much. I used to think my mom was crazy for worrying about me but now I'm afraid I'm going to be the same way with Ethan.

After I saw Benny I got a call from Christy.

"Listen, Jeff, if you've got a gripe about the way I'm taking care of Ethan, you talk to me straight out, don't go behind my back to Benny."

"I don't have a gripe. I just don't want Ethan in the car with Benny if Benny's been drinking."

"God! How stupid do you think I am? I'm not going to put Ethan in a car with someone who's been drinking. You come home from college to be the big dad and all of a sudden you know best? Who do you think took care of Ethan all those months you were away?"

"Okay, okay," I said.

"I'm not the little ninth grader who fell for you, Mr. Jeff Browning. I don't need you to tell me what to do. I'm not so stupid anymore."

"I never said you were stupid. I know you're not stupid."

"Well, I was stupid. I've learned a lot about myself through all this. I guess I thought if I just happened to get pregnant, that would mean you and I should be together. And if we stayed together, with a baby, I'd get your family and I wouldn't have to always be fighting with my dad. But it was stupid. I know now that I'm the only one who can make things better for me. I don't need some guy to do it for me."

"What about Benny?"

"We have fun together. He makes me laugh. But I'm not looking for him to take care of me. We don't see each other much, anyway."

"What about Dashan?"

"Dashan is one of my best friends in the whole world."

"But . . ."

"But none of your business. What about *your* private life?"

"I'm working on it," I said. We both laughed, and I felt the wall that had grown between us weaken.

I'm glad things are easier with me and Christy now. She's right that getting pregnant was a really stupid thing to do. And I was stupid, too, for letting it happen. But it's one of those things we can't go back and change, so we've got to make the best of it.

Anyway, trying to be one of those giant tree kinds of dads has totally changed my life. On days when I have Ethan I get him up about 6:30 so I can feed him and dress him and take him to the Infant Center in time for me to get to my first class at H.H.C.C.

I pick him up at 3:00, take him back to my house, then put him in his stroller and walk with him to the park. I show him birds and flowers, bushes and blades of grass, and I hold him on my lap on one of the swings and glide slowly back and forth. He likes that.

I remember that my dad used to bring me to this park and push me on these same swings, and help me down the tall slide, before he left us. I whisper in Ethan's ear, "I'll never leave you." I guess my whispers tickle, because he squeals and bounces on my lap. I watch some guys playing half-court basketball and wish, just for an instant, that I could join them.

I take Ethan home and give him dinner. He loves scrambled eggs and applesauce, so that's what we both eat. For dessert we have graham crackers. Then I give him a bath, put him in clean pj's, hold him while he takes his bottle, then lay him in his crib.

If I'm lucky, Ethan goes to sleep and I call Nicole, then work on school stuff. But sometimes he wants to stay up late and play, and if I don't pay attention to him he cries. Or sometimes he cries anyway. I hate those times, when I'm alone with him and he cries and cries, and I don't know what's wrong.

I got so frustrated once, when I'd done *everything*, including taking him for a ride in the car, that I left him screaming in his crib. I walked outside and banged my hand, hard, against the side of the garage. It hurt bad for a week. I didn't tell anyone about it, I felt so stupid. But the way I figure it, at least I didn't hit Ethan. I'd never do that.

Always before I go to sleep at night I think of my time at B.U. I mean it when I tell Ethan I'll never leave him the way my dad left me. I love him in the most pure way I've ever loved anyone, no strings. But as much as I love him, I can't help wishing Ethan could have held off about five years before he came into my life, instead of coming so soon. My life would have been better, and so would his. I'd have been a more grown-up father, already teaching, not struggling to make ends meet by working at a gym. And he'd have had a more grown-up mom, too.

I wish his mom could have been Nicole instead of Christy. I know that stuff about accepting what I can't change, but there are times I can't help wishing.

Late at night, when everything is quiet except for an occasional distant siren, or helicopter overhead, my soul wanders back to Brooker University. I smell the pine trees, and feel Nicole's soft warm body next to mine.

The lake, the old brick classrooms with wooden floors and hissing radiators, Mr. Slokum and the B.U. debaters, the student lounge, Kevin's collection of baseball caps strewn around our room—these images come to me in waves, and I ache for what I've missed.

Speaking of Nicole, she's coming to visit this summer, check out a few schools, and meet Ethan and my mom. I'll take her to Hollywood, and to the Chinese Theatre where she can see the stars' footprints imbedded in cement. I'm saving money so I can take her to Spago. Maybe we'll go to a club where movie people hang out. She says she wants to see the glamour. I remind her of *Grand Canyon*.

In a way Nicole and Brooker University seem like part of a dream life, and now I'm in my real life, with Ethan, back in Hamilton Heights. But I can hardly wait to see Nicky this summer, in reality. I hope we still love each other. I think we will.

Just as I'm getting all into how Nicole and I will still love each other, and how great it will be to see her again, the phone rings.

"Jeff?"

It's Christy.

"Ethan has a fever and the doctor wants to see him tomorrow. Can you take him?"

"Why can't you? Tomorrow's one of your days to have him."

"Yeah, but I'm scheduled to help with a field trip for my aide class. Mrs. Myers is depending on me."

"I've got a test tomorrow," I say.

We talk back and forth and finally figure out that I can go in early for my test. Christy doesn't have to be at the field trip bus until noon. She'll skip her early classes, then I'll pick him up and take him to the doctor. That's how our lives go some days. By the time I pick him up, his fever is gone, but I decide to have him checked out anyway.

While I sit with Ethan on my lap in the doctor's waiting room, watching kids who are older than he is playing around, I think of all he has to learn. He can sit by himself now. But he still has to learn to crawl, and walk, and talk, and throw a ball, and read. I can help him learn that stuff. And sex. He's going to have to learn about sex someday. I hope he won't start having sex too soon. I hold him on my lap, so he's facing me.

"Don't ever have sex with someone you don't respect," I tell him. "And don't ever have sex without a condom, even if the girl says she's on the pill."

"Goo," he says, grabbing my nose and hanging on.

"Hey!" I say, rescuing my nose from his grip. "Look at those fingers," I say, showing him his crooked pinkies. We laugh. I like that we laugh together. I turn him around so he can see the kids playing with blocks on the floor. He leans back against me. I think about how it felt to lean back against the oak tree at Brooker University.

However else my life turns out, I want to be giant tree strong for Ethan.

ABOUT THE AUTHOR

Marilyn Reynolds is the author of ***Detour for Emmy,*** an ALA Best Book for Young Adults. ***Detour for Emmy,*** the story of a 15-year-old who becomes pregnant, "vividly portrays teenage love and its consequences," according to *Publishers Weekly.*

Telling, Reynolds' first young adult novel, is the story of a 12-year-old girl who is sexually molested by the father of the children she baby-sits.

Reynolds is the author of numerous essays which have appeared in the ***Chicago Tribune, Los Angeles Times, Dallas Morning News, San Francisco Chronicle,*** and other national newspapers. Her work has also been published in literary magazines, professional journals, and anthologies.

Reynolds balances her time between writing, working with high school students, and keeping her back yard bird feeder filled. Her students help her keep in touch with the realities of today's teens, realities which are readily apparent in her novels.

She lives in Southern California with her husband, Mike. They are the parents of three grown children, Sharon, Cindi, and Matt, and the grandparents of Ashley and Kerry Ryan.

ORDER FORM

Morning Glory Press
6595 San Haroldo Way, Buena Park, CA 90620
714.828.1998; 1.888.612.8254   Fax 714.828.2049

			Price	Total
Novels by Marilyn Reynolds:				
___	*Love Rules*	1-885356-76-5	9.95	_____
___	Hardcover 1-885356-75-7		18.95	_____
___	*If You Loved Me*	1-885356-55-2	8.95	_____
___	*Baby Help*	1-885356-27-7	8.95	_____
___	*But What About Me?*	1-885356-10-2	8.95	_____
___	*Too Soon for Jeff*	0-930934-91-1	8.95	_____
___	Hardcover 0-930934-90-3		15.95	_____
___	*Detour for Emmy*	0-930934-76-8	8.95	_____
___	*Telling*	1-885356-03-x	8.95	_____
___	*Beyond Dreams*	1-885356-00-5	8.95	_____
___	Hardcover 1-885356-01-3		15.95	_____
	Breaking Free from Partner Abuse			
___		1-885356-53-6	8.95	_____
	Your Pregnancy and Newborn Journey			
___		1-885356-30-7	12.95	_____
___	*Your Baby's First Year*	1-885356-33-1	12.95	_____
___	*The Challenge of Toddlers*	1-885356-39-0	12.95	_____
___	*Discipline from Birth to Three*	1-885356-36-6	12.95	_____
	Teen Dads: Rights, Responsibilities and Joys			
___		1-885356-68-4	12.95	_____
	ROAD to Fatherhood: How to Help Young Dads			
___		1-885356-92-7	14.95	_____
___	*Surviving Teen Pregnancy*	1-885356-06-4	11.95	_____
___	*Safer Sex: The New Morality*	1-885356-66-8	14.95	_____
	Teen Moms: The Pain and the Promise			
___		1885356-25-0	14.95	_____
___	Hardcover 1-885356-24-2		21.95	_____
	Teenage Couples: Expectations and Reality			
___		0-930934-98-9	14.95	_____
	— *Caring, Commitment and Change*			
___	Paper 0-930934-93-8		9.95	_____
	— *Coping with Reality* Paper 0-930934-86-5		9.95	_____
___	*Will the Dollars Stretch?* Paper 1-885356-78-1		7.95	_____

TOTAL _____

Add postage: 10% of total—Min., $3.50; 15%, Canada _____
California residents add 7.5% sales tax _____

TOTAL _____

Ask about quantity discounts, Teacher, Student Guides.
Prepayment requested. School/library purchase orders accepted.
If not satisfied, return in 15 days for refund.

NAME _____ PHONE_____

ADDRESS _____

_____